The Guyanese Wanderer

The Guyanese Wanderer

Jan Carew

The Linda Bruckheimer
Series in Kentucky Literature

Sarabande Books

LOUISVILLE, KENTUCKY

Managing Editor
Sarabande Books, Inc.
2234 Dundee Road, Suite 200
Louisville, KY 40205

Library of Congress Cataloging-in-Publication Data

Carew, Jan R.
     The Guyanese wanderer : stories / Jan Carew. — 1st ed.
        p.   cm.
     ISBN-13: 978-1-932511-50-5 (pbk. : acid-free paper)
     ISBN-10: 1-932511-50-4 (pbk. : acid-free paper)
     I. Title.

     PR9320.9.C29G89 2007
     813'.54—dc22   2006029427

Cover image provided courtesy of the artist, Jan Carew

Cover and text design by Charles Casey Martin

Manufactured in Canada
This book is printed on acid-free paper.

Sarabande Books is a nonprofit literary organization.

THE KENTUCKY ARTS COUNCIL

The Kentucky Arts Council, a state agency in the Commerce Cabinet, provides
operational support funding for Sarabande Books with state tax dollars and
federal funding from the National Endowment for the Arts, which believes
that a great nation deserves great art.

Contents

Introduction

Jan Carew comes from that remarkable school of West Indian literature that moulds magic realism with poetic narrative, and this marriage is what provides the background to the stories in this brilliant collection, aided in addition by Carew's vast knowledge of life...by this I mean, quite simply, the understanding of the ordinary aspects of life, and his profound love of life. *The Guyanese Wanderer* is remarkable, too, because it provides the background for Carew's wide and deep knowledge of human nature. Carew mixes the mystical with the magical; he belongs to that distinguished group of writers, memorable amongst whom are Gabriel Garcia Marquez and Jan's countryman Wilson Harris; but Carew does more: he presents a stronger narrative line as the literary conveyor belt in his adoption of Latin-American surrealism, rather than the more single-minded mix of mystical and magical typical of the mode. This makes for a brilliant synthesis in Carew's writing.

The endorsement of country and place, context and environment, also gives strong meaning to Carew's stories. In "Tilson Ezekiel," the author's skill is shown in his enhancing the narrative by instilling into it what I call the context and the environment of the story in order to enrich the narrative itself:

> Darkness swallowed the sunset with a single gulp and stars scattered themselves across the skies like flocks of gilded rice-birds surprised by a scarecrow. The moon nudged its way above canopies of coconut palms and moonlight and smoke from Robert's pipe drove away the mosquitoes singing around his grizzled head. Navy blue shadows squatted under the trees like tethered beasts.

As the title of this collection states, the stories' literary strength is related to an acute knowledge and experience of someone who has traveled, not as a tourist, but as an investigator. The traveler's focus is on the landscape as much as it is on the relationship of the landscape to the people who occupy that landscape. We have, as a result of Carew's piercing observations of this slice of life, wandering through Guyana in the eyes of a Guyanese, and through his magical narrative, the best picture that can be drawn by a traveler. This is no flimsy, superficial, and cynically demeaning sentiment, as in the travel books of Vidia Naipaul's. Because this traveler is guided by maturity, in the literary and artistic observations that face him—and not the other way around!—this author as the camera, documenting what is given in the landscape and in the sociology of the people.

So, maturity—and also meant in the literal sense—a life spent in this observation of life—to be plebian—is measured with the eye of the artist to detail; and this might surprise many to know that Carew is a distinguished painter, whose canvases reflect the maturity of the eye—as analysis and as interpreter. In the same way, this eye stamps literary authority on the stories in this collection, and upon the subjects described with such authoritative precision that highlights the environmental context, just as a jazz drummer of the caliber of Elvin Jones elevates the drums from its historical function of a keeper of time, to this musical glory of integrated riffs and at the same time, a soloist instrument.

"Chantal" is a glorious story, in which the mature observer, sociologist, and painter draws a portrait of a woman that serves as a model and a moral standard of women's rights. It takes a man, and a writer, and a writer who is a man, to show Chantal, the man who loves this woman in her raw, tantalizing beauty, acknowledging moreover, "that there was not a man within a radius of three hundred miles of that vaginal centre who would not have paid the wages of two years of sweat and fear and terror in the gold and diamond mines in order to have her, and the knowledge was like a spot of venom in his brain." The man who describes this woman, in this tragic but beautiful manner, knows the power of a woman; and he witnessed, to his immediate disgust the manipulation that this woman displays toward a younger man, intent upon being her lover; intended to be a pawn in the web of her beauty and her wiles. And when this causes Chantal to behave like a "woman-owning" man, she strikes him down, physically; and pronounces her ownership over her body—remembering as we must, Chantal's own awareness of the power of her sensuality. But she is a modern-day woman, a liberated woman, and she reminds us this is the age of women's liberation, after she has knocked him cold with the flat part of a cutlass: "All-yuh, look after him. Ah didn't kill him, ah jus' sting him a bit.... From now on, I'm not Chantal's woman or any other man's woman. I'm my own sweet self, my own woman! Me, and me alone, will decide who I go out with, and when!"—and we can imagine her adding, "and what I do when I go out with who I go out with!"

That some of the stories are recognizably autobiographical is not to introduce a point of frivolous speculation of discovering similarities between details of the author's life and the text, but to comment upon the author's manipulation of these "experiences," and how he "changes" the incidents into an artistic new canvas upon which he defines, through his literary eye, the interior meaning—the *true* meaning that his observation has lifted from the ordinary vision to the rearrangement of those "experiences" through the eye that transforms their significance from the ordinary literary photograph, into art.

"Hunters and Hunted" demonstrates Carew's style and especially his powerful skill of narrative: "Tonic, his legs round Tengar's waist and his hands locked around his neck, looked like a black spider clinging to a tree trunk." And it is this powerful descriptiveness that justifies my point that Carew does not regard background and environment as a backdrop to a play, for example, but as a functioning integral part of the narrative itself—the literary force that propels the story. There is always the fierceness of beauty of the Guyana landscape, virginal still and untouchable, unconquerable perhaps, for the hunter and miner, untouchable in spite of the hunter's rifle, and the cries and shrieks of the hunted. The horror of the jungle, and the frightening darkness and the symbolic meaning of that darkness, come at us like the attacking brutal forces of darkness, and we, the reader, live through this fear, just as Tengar does, when he sees Tonic's "eyes looked like eggs in a dark nest."

The Guyanese Wanderer is, in another sense, an odyssey of the author's reminiscence of his experiences beyond the Guyana jungle and the Guyana hinterland to a way-station of European sophistication, nevertheless, a hollow one, in Paris, but as its cultural-ethnic realities demand, the psychic destinations—the terminus—must be the jungle of Guyana: the birthplace of this beauty and this wonderful landscape. I mentioned the author's maturity, meaning also the author's "age"—not in terms of calendar years, but his "position," his "place" in literature, both Guyanese and international, and I mean by this to put him into a "canon" that upholds his literary reputation, in other words, his universalist appeal. And no better example of this is to be found than in the bewitching, taunting delicacy of emotion, of sentiment, expressed in "Exile in Paris." When I read this story, I was in the same awe, in the same trance invoked by Jan Carew, as he told me parts of this odyssey which had taken him throughout the world, far from the thick beautiful inspirational soil of Guyana, and its still virginal beauty of landscape and possibility. The Guyanese Wanderer, thank god, is now home—again—after a successful journey.

Austin Clarke

The Guyanese Wanderer

THE VISIT

BELFON HEARD HIS MOTHER LOLA CALLING HIM: "Belfonnnnnnn! Belfonnnnnnn!" He was playing marbles with his friends between a cluster of chicken coops and a kitchen made of galvanized iron scraps and old petrol drums cut open and beaten flat. The hut and the kitchen were a patchwork of driftwood from the seashore, rusty metal sheets nailed to uprights, and rafters from which the bark had not been removed. Both the kitchen and the shack were raised on stilts to avoid the seasonal floods. But this makeshift hovel was the only home Belfon had known from birth, and there were times when the kitchen became a magical den from which tantalizing smells issued, and striking his nostrils, made his mouth water.

He was tall for his age, and often, suffered from attacks of "dark eyes" when pangs of hunger overcame him. The kitchen, with its covering of dark, unpainted wood and subdued, rusty hues, was also the abode of rats and cockroaches and chickens that were allowed free entry to prey on the cockroaches. And those chickens, cockroaches, rats, and the ever-present mosquitoes became folkloric characters that trickster heroes were always outwitting. But even though his young eyes never saw it as such, it was still a place of stinking cruel huts with intestines of rotting wood and rats, and yellowing newspapers sealing cracks and fissures; but it was also a place where feet danced and voices sang and raunchy tales were told, and transistors blared music at deafening decibels, and stray cats and dogs skulked around, ready to snatch scraps of food.

When Lola was happy, she brought sunshine into the yard with her laughter and teasing, and she'd hug her six-year-old son so tightly that he could feel her heart beating and smell the fragrance of her warm flesh. She taught him the art of survival by telling him proverbs. The two he always remembered were No matter how drunken Mr. Cockroach is, on his way home, he always gives chicken coop a wide berth. The other was Never cuss alligator till you done cross the bridge.

"Belfonnnnnnn! Belfonnnnnnn! But this little bad-john don't hear me callin' him!"

He came running and she hauled him off to the standpipe and gave him one of those baths that he hated. She used carbolic soap and her rough hands to scrub him from head to toe, and this ordeal was always the prelude to paying a visit to someone important in an affluent sector of the city. Between splashes of water from a calabash, he asked timidly:

"Where we goin' dis time, Mama Lola?"

"Going to see Mistress Elgin, boy. Got some business to discuss wid her."

Later, when the afternoon sun stretched their shadows behind them, he and Lola parted the hibiscus hedge in the Elgin back garden, and, crouching low, emerged from a tunnel of leaves and branches and flowers that dogs and children had made. It was the dry season and the pistils of the hibiscus flowers hung like parched tongues. A pack of dogs rushed at them, but the slum-yard had taught them how to deal with the hungriest and meanest dogs in the city, and instinctively they bent down swiftly as though to pick up rocks. The dogs, recognizing the gesture as one that could spell trouble for them, kept their distance until an Amerindian boy called them and asked:

"What you want, lady?"

"I want to see the mistress," Lola said, and deciding that the rude Amerindian boy wasn't even worth a thimbleful of her anger, she laughed. Belfon carried the sound of his mother's laughter with him throughout his life, for it always came as easily as water gushing out of a spring and it was akin to music. The Amerindian boy looked at them contemptuously, and his narrow eyes, bright as polished obsidian, seemed to be asking: What's this knock-about woman and her mauger-dog son doing in our yard? The small-boy was cleaning his teeth with his tongue because he'd been feasting on wild blackberries earlier on. Lola looked down at Belfon and said sharply:

"Belfon, close you mouth, nuh! You like some damn fly-catcher."

The Amerindian boy found this funny and guffawed, showing his big, yellow teeth until Lola turned to him wrathfully and added:

"What you standing there and skinning your teeth about? You deaf or something? What happen, you living here or you only a bird of passage like me?"

"What you want to see the mistress about, lady?" the Amerindian boy asked, stubbornly.

"But this lil buck-boy bold-faced, eh! What I want to see the mistress about? Boy, go 'long and inform the mistress that Lola want to see her," and when the Amerindian boy was turning around slowly to obey, Lola attached a rider to her request which shocked him, "Tell the mistress she knows me from prison."

"Mother! Mother!" he called out, running toward the big house. Lola noticed that her son was lagging behind her, and with a surprising gentleness, she said, "Come on, boy, what you 'fraid for?"

A voice answered from inside the house, "Yes, Simon, I'm here!"

"Mother, there's a woman here to see you, she say her name is Lola, and that you know her from prison!"

The old woman had come to the back door, and she reprimanded Simon, "Speak properly, boy! She say?"

"She says," Simon corrected himself.

Kathleen Elgin walked with a limp, and a cloud of white hair framed a pleasant brown face that old age had dented like a walnut. She wore bifocal spectacles, and it fascinated the child to see her eyes swimming behind them. Her cook, a small black woman with a moon-face and oriental eyes, chuckled and said in an undertone:

"Like one of you jail-people come to visit you, mistress." The heat in the kitchen was so intense that beads of perspiration hung like miniature stalactites from her brow.

"Lola, what good wind blow you this way, girl? I only see you when some kind of trouble befalls you," Kathleen Elgin said, smiling benignly.

"I too glad to see you, mistress. When you used to come and visit us in jail, you was like an angel from Heaven. Is not big trouble this time, mistress. How you do? You looking well," Lola said with an easy familiarity.

"I'm managing by the grace of God, girl. Who is that, your child?" Kathleen Elgin said; and, looking at her eyes moving like wavelets in a pond behind her bifocals, the small-boy was terrified.

Lola tugged at his arm and ordered, "Say good morning to the mistress, boy!"

"Morning, mistress," the boy said in a barely audible voice, as he stepped forward and extended his hand.

"Come inside and talk to me, Lola. I must get on with my sewing," Kathleen Elgin said. "And, Ida..." she turned to the cook.

"Yes, mistress, I know. I'll give the small-boy a glass of milk and some bread and cheese," the cook said.

"Simon, go and finish your work. The devil finds use for idle hands, boy," Kathleen Elgin said to the gawking Amerindian lad; and, the child was relieved because he didn't fancy having his snack with the older boy's eyes on him all the time. But, he could still hear Lola's voice clearly, and what she was saying robbed him of his appetite:

"Mistress, I expecting again, and I can't keep Belfon...he like a kinnah to me, mistress. I love him, but I gotto let him go. Ah can't keep on putting food in his belly and clothes on his back. The boy wearying mi spirit. He's six going on seven, and he growing wild like a tigercat...he got brains to do everything that's bad...ah send him to mi half-sister on the Courentyne, and he run away...ah send him to mi auntie in Essequibo, and he run away again...he say that all they was doing was working him hard and beating him...ah met an English soldier-boy, and he love me too much, mistress...he want to marry me...ah told him that Belfon was mi sister's boy-child..."

"You lied to him about something so important, Lola? That's hardly the way to start building a lasting relationship, girl," Kathleen Elgin said sternly.

"Ah couldn't bring myself to tell him the truth, mistress...I need a break, and this Belfon like a tick under my arm..." Lola began explaining, but the child, spilling his milk on the kitchen floor, rushed out, and embracing her fiercely, begged:

"Mama, Lola, don't send me away from you...ah will be good, I swear ah will be good...I swear..." His voice broke, and a storm of sobs shook his young body.

The old lady, with hair as white as morning mists on the river, signaled Lola to come closer, and when she obeyed, put an arm around her shoulder and a comforting hand on Belfon's head. The other children she had adopted had come with their fear and their silence, but this one, she thought, was a fighter. He was not going to allow a ne'er-do-well mother to cast him aside as if he were a household pet that had become a nuisance.

"He's a fighter," she said, fumbling for a handkerchief to wipe away a tear, "and he can stay with us, but you'll have to move in with us for a while, until he gets accustomed to this house and the other children."

Kathleen Elgin said this, knowing that in a day or two, Lola would disappear and return to her English soldier-boy and her wild, catch-as-catch-can life.

"Mistress, I can't tell you..."

"Don't say another word, Lola," Kathleen Elgin commanded, holding her head higher and pursing her lips.

Belfon stole a look at her, and wiping the remnants of his tears away with his knuckles, he kept thinking, *I wonder what this grand lady in the big house meant when she said I was a fighter. It sounded almost like praise.*

In the midst of his fear, bewilderment, and grief, he felt his heart pounding. And this stirring inside him was the same that a young harpy eagle feels when he flaps his wings and tests the wind long before he's ready to soar.

TILSON EZEKIEL
ALIAS TI-ZEK

HE'D BEEN DRINKING DHARU ALL DAY LONG with Ramkissoon, a cattle rustler from the Maichony savannahs. Ram had the smell of fear coming off him like the stench from a ramgoat. There was a quality of heaviness about Ram as if he was born with weights on his spirit. He talked heavily and walked heavily and ate and drank heavily. By sundown, when the sky had long streaks of fire and smoke stretching from end to end of the horizon, Ram was drunk and repeating the same story he'd been telling since morning.

"Boy, Ti-Zek, was cat-piss-and-pepper!" Ram's eyes were so red they looked like hibiscus petals.

Ti-Zek, reclining on a bed of banana leaves said derisively, "All-you too blasted stupid! Three grown men going to thief cattle in broad daylight from Singh ranch? All-you must've had too much bad-run in, all-you damn head. That was suicide, pardner! Don't tell me you didn't know was Buddy ranch! Government call in the guns an' yet Buddy got more guns than you got thirst for drink, and what's more he can use them. That man can hit a twenty-five-cent piece at fifty yard."

"Buddy is a douglah like you, Ti-Zek," Ram mumbled.

"Whatever kind of blood he got in him is bad blood, an' it mix with poison. That bitch more bad than a snake in the grass."

"Ti-Zek, tell me something, how come you get that rass name?"

"If I tell you, you won't believe me."

9

"Try me."

"Why you never ask me this question before? I done know you gone on fifteen years, and now all of a sudden you burst the question over mi head."

"Never wanted to know before."

"Mi mother wanted to have a name that nobody else had. So she christen me Tilson Ezekiel."

"And who cut it down to Ti-Zek?"

"Mi self nuh!"

Ram changed the subject, and said reflectively, "Buddy resemble you, you know, Ti-Zek. Sometimes me can't tell who is who."

"You jumping from one cofufflement to the other like a grasshopper in a bush fire, Ram. One or two rass drink in you head an' you can't talk sense, nomore!" Ti-Zek sucked his teeth contemptuously. "If I know Buddy, he let you get away an' he shoot them other two unablers you had with you for sport."

"When the bullet hit Charlie, he spin like a leaf in the wind. Charlie turn a leaf spinning in the wind. Charlie boy, rustling was not for you, old man! Should've stick to pragging. Prags, boy, prags! The whole country livin' by prags." Ram leant his leonine head to one side and rolled his inflamed eyes.

"And how Jag go, Ram?" Ti-Zek asked, although he already knew.

Ram pretended to be too drunk to understand the question. He didn't want to talk about Jag's death or the way he himself had escaped swimming across the Maichony River, while scores of alligators basked on the muddy banks eyeing him malevolently. Scores? Well, perhaps there were only a few, but they looked like scores.

"Jag was a rass," he muttered. "A real rass."

Day cleaned with a suggestion from Ram that they do a job on Boodoo's estate together. And having made the suggestion, alcoholic fumes rose in Ram's brain like incense. He kept thinking in this state of euphoria that he should go to Arjune, the Sadu, for a good luck charm to tide him over his current spell of bad luck, but Ti-Zek drove the thoughts from his mind with a burst of harsh banter.

"Do a job with you, Ram? Don't mek sport. you brain an' you frame too slow to keep up with me, pardner. And besides I like to work alone, all alone with my own sour self."

"I broke man, an' desperate, an' mi-chile mother threatening to take me to court."

"Which chile mother, Ram? I thought you lost count of the woman them who mother pickny for you."

"You gotto help me, Ti-Zek."

Against his better judgment Ti-Zek decided to join Ram in shifting a couple hundred coconuts from Boodoo's estate.

It was noontime. Low rain clouds were sifting the sunlight. The wind had vanished from the foreshore and was skulking somewhere deep in the forests. A pair of bluesakees were playing mating games in a low thicket of black sage and ant bush. They darted from one clump of bushes to the other and their wings were the color of bluebells.

Ti-Zek and Ram had picked the dry coconuts and were peeling them on iron spikes they had driven into the ground. They worked quickly. The job had to be done before the Rangers resumed their patrols after breakfast.

But Roberts, a bitter old man and the bane of raiders, had been tipped off by the rum shop owner who had heard Ram mumbling his secrets aloud between sleeping and waking. Roberts should have retired a long time ago, but a passion for hunting men kept him alive and on the job. For him, retiring to a quiet life would have been worse than death.

The first shot caught Ram in the back of the head, and falling forward, his own spike pierced his throat. Ti-Zek ran bird-speed zigzagging so that Roberts couldn't take proper aim. Two buckshot pellets caught him in the right leg, one close to the Achilles' tendon and the other in the big outer muscle of the thigh. Roberts made a gesture of pursuit but soon gave up, cursing himself for his age and decrepitude. He left Ram's body on the spike and went for help. He knew that Ti-Zek was bold and vengeful.

"That Ti-Zek like a Maipuri tiger," he said to himself as he walked away. "You frighten him and he will take a roundabout trail and come right back to ambush whatever make him run away." Ti-Zek, as Roberts had suspected, ran in a wide circle and returned to the spot where Ram had fallen. He himself was bleeding but had traced his wounds to their sources and was satisfied that they were only superficial ones.

"Jesus Christ, Ram had bad luck! Mantop was hunting him down for the whole of last month. Peculiar how Mantop does play games with some people before he snatch them, and I swear he was playing a tiger and bush rabbit game with ole Ram. Two times in three months Mantop make a pass at Ram. During December rains a boat engine exploded on the Mahaica River and toss him twenty-foot in the air. He had a bad back for months after that. Then Buddy shoot them two unablers who was rustling cattle with him, and now, the third time, old man Roberts, half-blind and decrepit, erase his name from the register of the living."

Ti-Zek watched Roberts hurry away noisily with his double-barreled shotgun cradled against his chest.

They say that Roberts can palaver with the dead, that he can gaff with jumbies on moonlight nights when he's alone in shadowy and silent coconut groves.

Ti-Zek didn't mind ghosts. What frightened him was the thought of being caught in a web of prison and desolation by one of those unfree spirits forever hunting him down.

He suppressed a feeling of revulsion, removed Ram's body from the spike that held it fast, laid it on the ground, and covered it with banana leaves. Above him the sky was the color of a buck-crab's back—a hard metallic blue—and carrion crows were already circling, floating on air currents and tracing patterns as though invisible, and deft hands were using them to write a secret calligraphy.

Ti-Zek, crouching in the shadows, waited around as long as he dared. He didn't want the carrion crows to rob Ram of his eyes, because Ram was the kind of man who always needed to see where he was going.

Long before he had stumbled into this unexpected and sudden exit of death, Ram had declared, "Pardner, me don't want to go to Heaven. Them say the big chibat does feed you on milk and honey there. That will only be a lotta work for me man, milking cow and goat, carrying them out to the pasture, sitting up all night to protect them from vampire bats. And who going keep the beehive, and gather the honey, and have bee stinging them and shutting up they eye? No, pardner, give me hell anytime! With all them friends and enemies down there, me will only have to work a two-hour shift a day stoking fire."

"So go well, Ram, I will miss gaffing with you. Remember that story you tell me 'bout this big chibat, who, when his first son born decide that the boy-chile should have the most reliable company in the world to grow up with? How this big chibat search and search and wrack he brain till he come up with the bright idea that the most reliable companion on this earth was Mantop? So he search out Mantop and say, 'Mantop, I want you to stand godfather for mi one-boy.' And Mantop say, 'All right, but there will come a time when I will have to come for him like everybody else.' And the boy father say, 'Well, that's you and he story. All-you two will have to settle that when the time come.' So Mantop become godfather for the boy, and the boy become the village doctor. Now, as a doctor, he see Mantop the Reaper come for old and young, weak and strong, rich and poor, and he keep thinking, 'All right, so Mantop is mi godfather. The two of us close as sweat to skin. I wonder if he will come for me the way he does come for everybody else?' So the doctor ask him, 'Mantop, why you don't make me you pardner for all time?' 'Can't do that,' Mantop say. 'Is only room for one of us in this job.' So the doctor go away, and from that time he start to learn all of Mantop tricks: how to enter a house anytime of day or night. An' Mantop, seeing how smart this doctor trying to get, decide to come for him before his time was up. The night Mantop come, the doctor get a real fright and he brain start to work overtime. When the quaking inside him abate, and he could find he tongue and give voice again he say, 'Godfather, give me two more days to settle up mi affairs, then you can come!' And Mantop agree. But as soon as Mantop leave the doctor get busy, and seal up every crease and crack and crevice in the house, board and bar the windows, and all he lef' open was one keyhole and he put a bottle to that keyhole and wait. Mantop come again jus' like he say, and when he see that he godson seal up everywhere he get vex like hell, an' he call out, 'Godson, open up this minute!' but the doc didn't answer. Well, wasn't long before Mantop find the keyhole and slip in and land right inside the bottle, and the doc jump up and seal him in, and although he cry out to make stone weep, the doc take the bottle and bury it in he back garden. Well, with Mantop gone, the doc act like he own land and sky, and he make mirth with anyone who try to stand in his way. He rob people of they land; he take 'way they wife and daughter; he properly parade himself and take advantage. But he didn't know that with Mantop gone, time stop and wait till he come back so nothing new was happening day in and day out. The doc was jus' stumbling round and round, walking the same trail in circles, till he get fatigue. And one day, when he couldn't think of nothing better to do, he start planting vegetables in the back garden, forking up the ground, and he break the bottle that had Mantop locked up. Mantop didn't wait then; he strike at once and carry the doc away.

"Well, old man Roberts give you a quick passage to the Beyond, pardner, so you an' you friends will do shift-work stoking fire down below. Go 'long you merry way, boy! I gotto go bird-speed. I can hear them coming. At least I save your eyes, Ram, so you can see where you going. And these two buckshot in mi leg biting me. I will send message to Sister Rhona an' ask she to come and fix it. She got a healing hand, and she will boil up some bush and in no time the wound will heal."

They came with dogs. Ti-Zek made a detour to the main canal and swam as quietly as an alligator for half a mile to ensure that the dogs would lose his scent.

Old man Roberts said, "Eh, eh, somebody move the body."

"Is that damn thief-man Ti-Zek," a young Ranger with muscles up to his ears said. "I wish you caught him instead."

"Is fifty-odd years I work on this estate, boy, and in all that time there never was a thief like Ti-Zek." Old Roberts spoke as though he had a profound respect for Ti-Zek, and this surprised the younger Rangers.

The musclebound one said, "Me will get him sometime, man."

But Roberts cautioned him, "Don't bite off more than you can chew, boy; learn the Ranger work, and study Ti-Zek like a book, read every sign he lef' behind him, and if you suspect he around, every blade of grass that move might not be the wind moving it; it might be Ti-Zek waiting to ambush you. I wish I had Ti-Zek as a Ranger. This estate wouldn't lose a single coconut."

They made a stretcher out of plaited coconut branches and carried Ram's body to the threshing floor of a rice mill that had long been abandoned to rust and moss and rats and sleepy serpents. Narine walked slowly down the pathway from his house leaning heavily on a gnarled letterwood stick. He approached the corpse and prodded it with his stick, and staring ahead of him his eyes became calm and contemplative.

Here was a thief shot in the act of robbing him of the rightful fruits of the land he had inherited from his ancestors! He wished that the soul of this lost one, this spawn of Kali the Destroyer, could migrate for an eternity from the body of one wild beast to another. He stood there for such a long time that the others around him became restless and uncomfortable. Ram's brains, pouring out from the back of his head, looked like fallen petals of a yellow hibiscus, and this viscous pulp almost touched the toes of Narine's shoes.

Roberts cleared his throat loudly, and looking up from his daydream Narine ordered one of the young Rangers to go and fetch the Police, "Boy, make sure you find Inspector Gordon. Tell him that Uncle say he must come right away."

"I will find him," the Ranger said. "I not coming back with nobody else."

The Inspector was a big man who walked as softly as an ocelot. He had a thick neck and the veins on it stood out like lianas; but even when he was as hearty as a red howler monkey in the mating season, one was conscious of his small eyes, and how cautious they were, and how sly and cunning they could be, and how absolutely they belied his apparent joviality. Standing beside Narine with the sun behind him the Inspector looked like a dark boulder shielding a blade of grass.

"Gordon, I too glad to see you, man, too glad." Narine extended a hand that was veined and fragile and trembling like a leaf in a gentle wind.

The Inspector took the small and vulnerable hand in his immense one, and declared, in a voice that sounded like the roll of drums, "Came as soon as the boy came and told me you had some trouble here, Uncle. I was on my way to settle a disturbance in Baggotstown. Is human-beast we have to deal with these days, Uncle."

The Inspector exchanged a few pleasantries with Roberts whose deceased wife had been a distant relative of his, and then he took out his notebook and began to question him officially. Roberts gave a rambling description of what had transpired and the Inspector, again and again, brought him back to the main point. Narine listened so impassively that the flies crawling on the face of the corpse and those on his own face seemed to be crossing the same surfaces of dead flesh.

The young muscular Ranger was anxious to give his version of what had happened. He felt that he could do a much better job than Roberts, but a look from the old landowner was enough to let him know that the choices were his silence or his job.

"It's clear as rainwater that Ram and Ti-Zek was working together, Inspector. Them two was always close as sweat to skin and..." Roberts would have continued.

But the Inspector interrupted him, "Leave Ti-Zek out of this, Roberts!"

"Leave him out, Inspector?" Roberts looked up, and his big veined eyes sunk in wrinkled flesh were wide open with bewilderment.

The Inspector smiled and explained patiently, "Come, come, Roberts, old man, a black man and an Indian joining forces to rob a notable landowner? No, sir, that's politics. My job is to uphold the law, to deal with crime. So here is what the official story will be, and this will be the whole truth and nothing but the truth et cetera: Ram was caught red-handed stealing coconuts at ten-thirty in the morning of April fifth. You and two young Rangers called on him to surrender, and you surrounded him. You called on him to give himself up peacefully three times. He took a few steps forward, as though he was going to comply, and then he picked up a cutlass and rushed at Ranger Telford. You shot him. With a story like that, everybody comes out looking good and there's no untidiness about the affair."

The Inspector's eyes made four with each of the Rangers in turn and they nodded their agreement and lowered their heads.

"Come to the house and have a drink, Gordon," Narine said. "Is a long time since you come this way, man."

"Glad to, Uncle," the Inspector said. And when they were out of earshot of the others, he added in a low voice, "There's a nice little piece of property in Georgetown that I have my eyes on, Uncle, and I'll need a mortgage."

"After all, is cooperation and self-help these days, Gordon."

"So what you want us to do with the body, Inspector?" Roberts called out.

"I'll notify the hospital as soon as I get to a telephone. They'll send an ambulance. Look out for the ants and the wild dogs and the carrion crows. Don't want to spoil things for the autopsy, you know."

Roberts watched the two walking up the pathway to the big house with its green gables and the darkness inside which often made Narine keep the lights on in the daytime, and he kept repeating under his breath: "The wild dogs and the carrion crows and the ants!" And he said to himself, "This is a place with vultures and creatures and things to back-up the vultures. Wild dogs and carrion crows and ants and cannibal fish."

"You say something, skipper?" the young Ranger asked.

And Roberts told him that he could go home to his wife and children since they all had a hard day. "I will keep vigil over the body," he said. "Never know when that ambulance will turn up."

Darkness swallowed the sunset with a single gulp and stars scattered themselves across the skies like flocks of gilded ricebirds surprised by a scarecrow. The moon nudged its way above canopies of coconut palms and moonlight and smoke from Roberts' pipe drove away the mosquitoes singing around his grizzled head. Navy blue shadows squatted under the trees like tethered beasts. The old man, with his shotgun across his knees, listened to rainfrogs crying out to the moon and who-you birds conversing with ghosts; and every now and then he swayed and nodded drowsily, murmuring strange orisons between sleeping and waking. Around midnight, he heard the chickens in his backyard coop, behind the rice mill, stirring restlessly. He stood up and shook himself and stamped the ground to banish the stiffness from his joints. Palm fronds, stirring fitfully in the wind, made rusty whispers echo in dark groves where owls and mice played secret games.

As if the wind and moonlight had filled him with the breath of life again, Ram stood up, shook himself like a wet dog and began walking away. Roberts, when he recovered from the shock and amazement and fear that had overcome him, called out and fired a warning shot; but Ram, looking back and covering the hole in his throat with his right hand, disappeared in the shadows.

Roberts felt himself floating down a river in his canoe until he struck a submerged log and the canoe capsized. He found himself swimming endlessly in opaque depths. When the ambulance arrived, the body had vanished and Roberts was in a coma. He never regained consciousness.

For months afterwards, the villagers kept telling stories of how this or that one had seen Ram and Roberts walking side by side, and how the two had always smiled a cunning secretive smile, and how Ram was forever covering the hole in his throat with his hand.

Sepersaud Narine died in his sleep six months later. His body, frail and floating in a sea of wild flowers, lay in state in the cool dark living room of the big house. A cluster of Pandits chanted prayers to the gods and their messengers in the Hindu Pantheon who would take the soul of the deceased back into an eternal web of transmigrations.

The cremation ceremony took place on the foreshore in midafternoon when the tide was low and the wind was whispering requiems in the verging courida groves. The Pandit intoned and the distant sea and the wind and the mourners responded. Flames from the scented wallaba pyre bent the body in two. It looked as though the corpse was sitting up, defying the fire and at the last moment trying to cheat death. But those who attended the funeral swore they saw a hand reach into the flames, push the body backwards, and hold it down until it disintegrated.

Narine's heirs, as he had stipulated in his will, recovered his ashes and placed them in a marble urn in the center of his seventy-square-mile estate. The urn was surrounded by coconut palms, ant bush, black sage, and yellow acacia flowers.

The night after the urn was installed, Ti-Zek drove an iron spike close to it and carried out a ritual of stripping hundreds of coconuts so that the husks obliterated the fading wreaths piled on the ground. As Ti-Zek worked, the moonlight striped the ground with shadows and who-you birds cried out malevolently to one another. He shelled the coconuts on the spike rhythmically and interspersed his actions with words.

"Uncle, how much land a man does need after all? You had so much that from your housetop to the end of the sky a man couldn't see all that was yours, and now all you can claim is enough earth to cover your blasted ashes. You had to leave all that land, and the money in the bank and the bad-mindedness to crush other people lives in you weak trembling hand. When Mantop come for you, in you sleep, you couldn't offer him deeds to the land or cash in the bank, 'cause he is a dealer in life and death. So, Uncle, I working close to the miserable ashes they put in a stone jug, an' you can't do nothing 'bout it, an' you Rangers them afraid of the moonlight and the jumbies and all them people who die on this estate with the taste of bile in they mouth and blood in they eye and emptiness in they heart 'cause they hurt so much they couldn't feel pain nomore. So I taking these coconut for all them mute folk who life you squeeze like simitu on a vine when you suck out the sap and throw away the skin, them people who gray-hair they life and toil like slave to make oil from you coconuts-them. Is only Ram and me get away from you; both of we free like the wind is free or a harpy eagle does be in the wide, wide sky, out of your reach. So let you ashes eat all the land it can eat and never rest in peace!"

The who-you birds called out more insistently, and the estate workers, listening inside their cruel huts, shivered and shut out the moonlight and the shadows and the rusty murmurings of wild palms.

The muscular young Ranger who had succeeded Roberts stumbled upon Ti-Zek's handwork on his foreday morning patrol, and making sure that his only witnesses were singing birds, he laughed until he cried.

CHANTAL

CHANTAL SAT UP IN BED AND LOOKED AT his woman asleep beside him, and a surge of revulsion swept over him at the way her body abandoned itself to the bed. She lay on her back with her right hand against her cheek, the fingers denting her soft skin and the heel of her palm twisting her mouth. The thin cotton sheet covering her naked body clung to her like an extra skin. Her legs lay carelessly apart and he could see the dark outline of pubic hairs under the sheet. He was sure that there was not a man within a radius of three hundred miles of that vaginal center who would not have paid the wages of two years of sweat and fear and terror in the gold and diamond mines in order to have her, and the knowledge was like a spot of venom in his brain.

She was the only woman who had ever bound him to her the way she did, and he both loved and hated her for it. She was intelligent, fiery-tempered, maddeningly sensuous, strong-willed, and contrary, but hers was, at best, a difficult beauty. She was tall and buxom with a proud neck and wide shoulders. She had never completely lost the folds of fat around her belly and back since giving birth to her second child, and her generous, shapely hips and long legs tapered down to small, parrot-toed feet. Her round ageless face with its flawless santantone complexion could reflect more swiftly changing moods than Guyana skies at the beginning of the rainy season. She also had the most expressive eyes Chantal had ever seen. They were big and golden brown, and they reminded him of honey cupped in balsa flowers and touched by morning sunlight. Those eyes of hers could spurt flame when she was angry, dazzle like springs, melt a man's heart when they were sad, or turn an ordinary chap into a wild beast when they became hooded and stubborn. Her hair, the color of raw gold, was tinted with red, and the hot-iron combs she used to straighten it made it shine like patent leather. Chantal became aware of her sweaty calf touching his leg, and he drew away from her.

Before getting out of bed, he looked at the mists over the river through the mosquito net. It was as though there were charcoal burners under the water, piling green logs on top of fires that had burnt all night, and the mist was the smoke from these fires. It was day-clean and the rising sun was sweeping away the darkness. From the high bluff on which his bungalow was perched he could not see the river, but he could hear it surging around the bend at Garraway Point, chafing against the rocky banks, hissing like the snake god in the gorge of Kaietuk, and he knew it had been raining heavily up-country. The high sierras of Akarai, Kanuku, and Pacaraima had forced the rain clouds to give back to the rivers, forests, and high savannahs, the moisture sucked out of them. And the clouds, freed from their burden, rose high above the mountaintops and drifted across the pastures of heaven. Climbing out of bed, and moving quietly around the bedroom as he was getting dressed, Chantal thought that the heavy downpours up-country would soon erase the golden sandbanks on the river where he had fished and sunned himself and dallied away lazy hours, and whirlpools and white water would take over.

A family of red howlers was roaring half a mile away, drowning out the occasional birdsong and the river's persistent lisping.

"She doesn't hear a thing," Chantal muttered. "She's just lying there with her mouth open like a blasted cannibal fish!"

He could see the glint of teeth between her parted lips; and they were small, even and white as tiger orchids. He thought, That mouth of hers, whether she's asleep or wide-awake, makes her look perpetually discontented.

A fretful wind was nudging the mists aside and shafts of sunlight were filtering through like incandescent fingers probing to find earth. Tall trees, their lower trunks hidden by billowing clouds of mist, seemed to have roots in a fallen sky. Chantal had ringed his farm with balsa trees, and in five years, the saplings he transplanted had grown fifty feet tall. At nights, he was sure he could hear the trees groaning as they reached for the sky, and he had often thought that if he could pile those balsa trees one on top the other, he could build a ladder to the stars.

In addition to the corn and root crops he had planted, birds and wild animals had seeded some of the ground he had cleared with guavas, pineapples, cashews, sugar apples, and sapodillas. He liked the flowers on his balsa trees. They grew directly out of smooth, cylindrical trunks and transformed themselves into perfectly shaped chalices that filled slowly with honey. In the early mornings, troops of monkeys would come and, picking the balsa flowers, hold them in their delicate hands. Then drinking the fermented honey wine, they'd tumble and chatter and make love until a snake or a jaguar pounced, ending their morning bacchanal and sending the drunken troupes fleeing like demented spirits into the depths of the forest. And echoes of their alarm would linger in the air long after they had disappeared.

Chantal had also planted a ring of coffee and cocoa trees around his bungalow. The cocoa flourished in the shadow of taller trees, and there was no smell as fragrant as that of coffee blossoms in the early morning when the air was heavy with dew. In the center of his concession, there was a Brazil-nut tree two hundred and fifty feet high, a monarch of the selva with a flowering crown that scraped the sky. And when the ground under this giant was littered with fresh fallen nuts, snakes—emerald-green boas, bushmasters, parrot snakes, labarias—would sweep them together with their tails and burrow inside the mounds they made to cool themselves and wait for unsuspecting prey. It was quite normal for Chantal to capture half a dozen snakes when he went to gather Brazil nuts. And quietly, without his woman seeing what he was doing, he would then set the snakes free in the bush beyond his balsa trees.

That Brazil-nut tree was in the center of a thousand-acre concession Chantal had leased from the Government. He had spent months cutting away the vines and creepers and parasite orchids that threatened to bleed it to death, and then he had built a tree house two hundred feet up. From this vantage point he could see a panorama of the Guiana heartland under a sky the color of a blue flame: the purple Pacaraima Mountains looked like gigantic tables at which the Carib gods could sit and gaff and feast; the moody Garraway Stream, still as a looking glass in places, or raging down staircases of rock in others, had dark water bursting into flowering cascades of foam, until its energy was spent and it subsided in quiet pools; or he could look at the sea of forests stretching toward the horizon where, calcined by the sun, it fused with the sky. On a clear day, he could make out the hills above the Tumatumari rapids and the neat, luminous green terraces that migrant farmers from the Caribbean islands had created. Beyond Tumatumari, there was an occasional hole in the canopy of flowering treetops, where some lone individual was pitting his energies against a continent of forests. From his high treetop perch, his eyes could also follow the course of Garraway Stream up to its confluence with the Karibrong and Potaro Rivers. In the dry season these rivers were strewn with sandbanks that looked like golden sovereigns that drunken porkknockers had cast aside. The Brazil-nut tree towered like a mainmast and flaunted its flowering pennants high above the sea of Potaro forests.

But Chantal's woman regarded this magical Brazil-nut tree, and the snakes under it, as harbingers of evil, and she always gave them a wide berth.

On several occasions, she had taunted him, saying, "That tree must've housed the devil-serpent in the Garden of Eden."

Once, when Chantal went away on a hunting trip, she had hired a gang of men to cut it down, but he had returned unexpectedly and sent the men away, and he had told her angrily, "It's not the tree you hate; it's me."

"Me? Hate you? Don't make me laugh! You're really smelling your sweat, Chantal," was her contemptuous rejoinder.

"You know how long it took that tree to grow big and tall like it is, Sweet-girl?" he asked, trying to be conciliatory.

"I don't care if the tree was here since Jesus wept for our sins. All I know is that my son Tiho is just starting to walk, and I don't want him straying under that bad-luck tree with all those snakes waiting under it to kill him."

"Tiho is a man-child and I'm teaching him how to take care of himself...you know that."

She was always bringing Tiho into their arguments. He was their seventeen-month-old infant who could barely blow his own nose. A chasm had yawned between them after Tiho was born, separating them inexorably, and he'd been trying in vain to get to the roots of this vexing alienation. He had hoped that the baby would drain the discontent out of her heart, bring them closer, but it had not worked out like that at all. Instead, he sensed in her a growing resentment, and a suppressed anger. It was as though he had inflicted a wound on her that would never heal. When she was in the throes of childbirth with that second child of theirs, he had held her screaming with pain and cursing him, and the screams had pierced his brain like red-hot daggers. He had tried to atone for the agony and mystery of childbirth that he felt he had inflicted on her by putting up with her long spells of brooding, her tantrums, her scorn; but, later, Tiho, clinging to her ripe breasts, sucking greedily, was like a shield she held between them.

Occasionally, when her discontent became unbearable, he had taken her to Amagan's shop at Kaburi, twelve miles down the road that wound its way past his farm. Porkknockers and their women were always there drinking, laughing, and swapping bawdy stories. This time, after a few drinks of white rum, the high-tension wires stopped jangling in her brain, and she relaxed and presided over the gathering like a queen. Amagan liked having her around; it was good for business.

A man from the city was there one evening when Chantal's woman was in charge and holding forth. He was in his early thirties and his manners were as smooth as his black satin skin. He had a full head of black curly hair, and it was clear that his sweet-man's face had seldom beaten against harsh suns and wind and weather, and that his soft body had never been brutalized by hard labor. His short, thick torso, mounted on sturdy legs, sported a bulging waistline, and words rolled off his tongue as if he had been brought up on birdseed.

Chantal, on the other hand, was lean and strong as a leopard, and there was an overriding aura of male arrogance about him as he strutted around. At first, he didn't seem to mind his woman flirting openly with the stranger. But as the night wore on he became irritated when he saw her looking into the man's eyes and laughing with that easy sensuous laughter that used to make his heart sing when he was courting her.

The carbide lamp that hung from a rafter was so bright that it turned the dark faces of the customers navy blue. Amagan sat on a high stool behind the bar, hunched like a king vulture, his smoky eyes taking in everything.

The whores, who were making a tour of the up-river districts during a lean season in Georgetown, had selected their partners for the night.

Toad had latched onto Gabriel, a young porkknocker from Issano, a slim, elegant boy who sported a Polaroid camera that was the envy of everyone from Mabaruma in the North to Lethem in the High Savannahs. Toad was an aging lady of delight, squat, big breasted, light on her feet, and with a tongue as sharp as an accouri thorn. When she laughed her chins distended themselves and shook like Jell-O. She was a devout Catholic, and went to mass and confession regularly.

Tokyo Rose had teamed up with Uncle Benjy, a laughing giant, slow and easygoing and incapable of anger. He was standing at the bar drinking whilst she leaned against him affectionately. She was half-Chinese and half-Negro, a delicate looking creature with a torso like a young boy, juicy hips and shapely legs. Beside Uncle B., she looked like a reed leaning against a giant mora. She was a dangerous woman to cross, for when she was angry she had all the fury and the venom of a jeweled Iguanaria snake.

Mary-hot-poke was black and shiny as an obsidian knife. Her white, sequined dress clung to her like latex, and her beauty was so flawless it was as though she had been fashioned by one of those Greek sculptors who borrowed what was best in a dozen models to create a single perfect image. Men paid her for her beauty, not her performance, which many of the regulars said was indifferent, and could not compare with Toad's. She had two old men in tow. One was tall and stiff and pompous with a neck as wrinkled as a turtle's, and the other, fat and wheezing, had the bulging watery eyes of a crocodile. But they were both loaded, and Mary preferred them to the young men with their hot hands and ardent sweet-talk who would keep her up all night, wanting to impress her with their marathon performances instead of the cold cash that she preferred.

Janet-bruck-iron, the senior member of the party, sat in a corner, away from the harsh light. Her face, once beautiful, now looked like parchment stretched tightly over a bleached skull, and when she tried to smile seductively at the young man opposite her, all she could manage was a leer. But she had breasts like granite and an indestructible body.

Marabunta Lucy stood at the bar, behind Uncle B., drinking the whisky old man Shark had bought for her. Shark looked like an effigy propped up on his expensive artificial legs (one leg had been amputated above the knee and the other below, after an accident in the gold mines). His face was smooth and black. Only his white hair and heavy-lidded eyes betrayed his age. Shark, who was nearly sixty, had the torso of a young man, a massive slightly rounded back, a powerful chest, and a small waist. Lucy, his companion, was a peasant girl from the coast who could not have been more than twenty. She was tall and sturdy, and her dazzling smile and shining cotton eyes lent an irresistible charm to a countenance that would otherwise have been ordinary.

The air around the carbide lamp was boiling with insects, and the haze they created softened its glare. A rainbow-colored moth, the size of a young breadfruit leaf, flew into the room and circled the lamp until, flying through a cloud of rainflies, it burnt one of its wings and fell to the floor. For a moment it lay still and then it began to flap around helplessly. Uncle B., who had taken off his boots, walked over and crushed it under a bare foot, and as he returned to the bar, he wiped his foot on the floorboards, leaving a pattern of stains behind him.

"Why you didn't leave it alone? That moth beautiful like rass, man," Amagan said. "Tobesides, you mek a mess of mi-shop-floor."

"Beautiful? Lemme tell you, I had a good hunting dog, couple years back, and he ate one of them moths and died," Uncle B. said. "They look pretty, but they poisonous like hell."

"You must've been starving the blasted dog," Amagan said, and everyone laughed.

"I remember that dog," Shark said. "You used to call him Lion of Judah."

"Lion of Judah was a brave dog. I used to hunt tigers with him," Uncle B. said, looking at his drink thoughtfully and tossing it down his throat with a practiced ease.

"Let's have some music!" Chantal's woman said, and as soon as the words left her mouth Gabriel took out a flute, Amagan fetched a bongo drum and a guitar, and Uncle B. took the guitar from him and sat on the bar.

"Let's have some bright music...like the old days, eh, Amagan!" Shark said. Amagan sat on his high stool with the bongos between his knees. Uncle B. tuned the guitar and struck up a lively, catching tune. Amagan and Gabriel joined in. Chantal's woman pulled the stranger to his feet and said, "Let's dance." But first, he looked at Chantal, bowed deferentially, and asked, "Mind if I dance with your woman?"

He felt uneasy with these men from the forest. They had something quiet and deadly about them. He also knew that although they might quarrel and fight amongst themselves, they would join forces instantly against an outsider. Whilst Chantal's woman, with her face flushed and her eyes as bright as dewdrops, was spinning an enchanted web around him, he could sense the disapproval of the men, and the open approval and solidarity of every female in the room with Chantal's woman. This reluctant swain from the city, caught in the middle of a collective male-female contest of wills, felt a noose tightening around his neck. He responded to the pressure by downing snap-glasses of white rum, and whenever his eyes made four with Chantal's, his faint heart wriggled like a trapped guppy fish.

Chantal was built like a Watusi warrior. When he stood up, he held himself so erectly that he gave the impression of being taller than he really was. He combed his hair straight back, and the comb left parallel grooves in the coarse wiry tuft in front. He had a high forehead, a long big nose, and full lips that curved like a bow at the corners. His big, gentle eyes never looked at you directly. It was as though a veil of dreams always separated him from other people, and those who did not know him well often mistook this for shyness or disdain. The doleful expression on his face was seldom an accurate guide to his moods though, for he could look sad or forbidding even when he was happy. Looking at him one knew that he was absolutely in control of both his body and his mind, and yet there was something baffling and impenetrable about his personality, as though both his Amerindian and Negro ancestors had burdened him with a heritage of secret dreams gathered in the forests of two continents. It was obvious to the stranger that the others respected Chantal, and looked on him as their leader.

"You can dance with her as much as you like," Chantal said, feigning an air of casualness, and looking away from them both.

"Thank you Mr. High-and-Mighty," his woman said sarcastically, with a nod of her head.

"Why you harassing the man so?" Shark chided.

"Me? Harassing him?"

"Yes, you . . . don't push Chantal too far, gal."

Shark thought he was offering the advice like a father speaking to an unruly child.

"Leave her alone!" Chantal called out above the music.

"Don't say I didn't warn you," Shark said, but the woman acted as if she hadn't heard him. She was already dancing, pressing herself close to her reluctant partner, mesmerizing him with the rhythmic movements of her body.

Watching the two of them, Shark continued under his breath, "Why you letting yourself fall into this trap, a sensible man like you? Can't you see this woman is a teaser? Man, she won't even tell you her name. She will lead you right up to the entrance of her house of treasure and then slam the door in your face. After all these years of hustling you should've known better . . . can't you see Chantal is a killer? Just look at the way he wears his prospecting knife strapped to his waist! All you came to Kaburi to do was to clinch a deal with Amagan, sell him some hot goods you picked up in Georgetown. So, pardner, when this dance finish, you better jus' leave the woman alone and hot-foot it to your bed in the back room."

The woman sensed her partner's growing uneasiness and despised him for it. But she felt a nagging rage against Chantal. Why am I doing this? she asked herself, but she could not answer the question. The five years that she and Chantal had been man and wife had tied them in a web of habits and hidden animosities, and she had, somehow, always been the one to give in, to compromise. But tonight, she told herself, ah feel like some kindah pocomania's taken me over, and this powder-puff of a man from the city who I don't really give a damn about, is the one triggering it. She smiled broadly to herself as she savored a strange atavistic pleasure and an urgent need to assert her freedom—the freedom of her limbs, her mind, her being! The stranger tossed down a drink of white rum and they continued dancing. She felt his hot alcoholic breath on her neck, and as he held her tighter, she told herself amusedly that sometimes in a crisis, fear and lust and rum could make even a small, timid man act like tiger.

Chantal was fearless when it came to facing danger or dealing with other men. He had the courage born of years of pitting his strength and cunning against the forest. He had even gone to the country of the black leopards in the Kanaku and Pacaraima sierras that the bravest of the Acewayo and Carib hunters had avoided from time immemorial. For they claimed it was the country of the Amerindian devil-spirit, the Kanaima, and they had heard that those who had ventured there before had been seized by the Kanaima, and to deter any other trespassers, a poisoned thorn was stuck into their tongues, their anal tubes pulled out and tied into a knot, and the victims had died slowly, their bodies becoming as bloated as a drowned tapir's. When Chantal returned unharmed from his journey to the country of the black leopards, the Indians renamed him Kabo-Tano, the Chosen One, and his fame had spread as far as the Amazon and the Orinoco.

But she, his wife of five years, had lived with him long enough to discover where he was most vulnerable. She knew how lonely he was, how frightened he was of being thought of as having human fragilities like everyone else. There were nights when he had come to her full of self-pity, and whimpering like a leopard cub, he'd declared he was a failure, that after his four years in the army and his eight years abroad studying and working, his return to Garraway Point was a retreat beyond the edge of darkness, an escape into the womb of the forests. And she had comforted him, holding him against her bosom and rocking him to sleep. She knew how much he needed her, and because his need was so great, it had imprisoned her during the best years of her life. He and Tiho and Asota, the two children she had by him, had robbed her of the pristine beauty that was hers when she was in her twenties, and drained some of the life force from her being. Long ago, her virago of a mother, with her witch's intuition, had warned her about Chantal.

"Leave that nigger-man alone. He's got a curse on his head. Every time he comes near me mi-heart goes all cold inside me."

And she had been noticing of late, too, now that he had vampired all that was best out of her, his eyes were straying to younger women.

The music made her feel as if she had been chewing cocoa leaves. It was as if she was floating on the cool bosom of a river.

She whispered to the stranger, "He's going to town tomorrow..."

"Who?"

"My husband...you must come after dark..."

"But...but...Marina..." He couldn't find the words to tell her about the myriad fears besetting him. He knew that the moment he left Amagan's shop everyone would know where he was going, and what would he get out of it? He had been around with other men's wives long enough to know that with twenty-four hours to brood over what she was planning to do, she could change her mind. Looking at her closely he could see that she was on the brink of hysteria, her hair was in disarray, and her eyes burning as if she had fever.

He muttered to himself, "Jesus! Why I didn't glue my backside to a bench, get pissed, and creep into my bed!"

"You going to come, Dodo?" she asked softly.

"Yes, I'll come," he lied, knowing full well that at the crack of dawn, he'd be hopping on the first lorry heading for Bartica. And he mused, Ah can jus' see myself crawling through miles of jungle from Kaburi, and if I get past the tigers and snakes and Jesus in Heaven knows what else, I'll creep up on this woman's veranda to stop a bullet. No sir, not me! Come to Georgetown anytime, Sweet-girl, I'll be waiting for you.

Chantal, standing behind them, interrupted his musings.

He said to his woman, calling her by her name for the first time, "Let's go, Beltina!"

The music stopped and couples walked back to their tables. "I'm not ready to go home yet," Beltina said, holding on to the stranger's arm. Chantal caught her by the wrist and flung her toward the open doorway. She stumbled over a bench and lay sprawled out, face down on the floor. Shark walked over to her stiffly and helped her to her feet.

"You were asking for trouble," he said, and she spun around quickly and spat in his face. Then she sat hunched and silent on a bench for a while.

Chantal and the stranger faced each other. The man was smiling stupidly and turned to make a quick exit. Chantal whipped out a bull-pistle and struck him across the back. The stranger, in the act of running away, froze in his tracks, his arms raised above his head and his eyes dilating. The next blow relaxed him until he felt his knees giving way under him. He screamed and whimpered like a wounded baboon.

Frog and the other whores gathered around Beltina protectively, and Uncle B. grumbled, "The bastard wouldn't even fight back . . . ah don't understand that kind of young man. Whoever make him filled him with jellyfish instead of guts . . ."

The stranger staggered toward the bar, and bracing his back against it cried out: "Jesus of Nazareth be mi-witness, I didn't do this man nothing and still, he beating me like a snake. All-you take my word for it, Dodo Martin never going to forget this till his dying day . . . and, Mr. Chantal, don't ever come to Georgetown, because I will make it so hot for you there, you will wish you was never born."

Gabriel guffawed and said, "Uncle B., who say the man don't have guts? Just hear how he threatening Chantal."

Amagan said, passing him a snap-glass full to the brim, "Have a drink of white rum, and then go on back to bed; you had a full day."

The stranger gulped the drink down, and Amagan added, "You better take the bottle with you and give your back a rubdown before you sleep; that bull-pistle does leave you with the mark of Cain."

Chantal walked up to the stranger and said, "I will come to Georgetown anytime I feel like it, and I will bring my woman along so that the two of you can continue your love game." He turned toward Beltina. The women were still clustered around her.

"Yuh coming, Beltina?" he called out, and turning to face the door, waited with his back toward her.

Shark said, "Don't do nothing stupid when you get home now, Chantal; enough is enough!"

The stranger took off his embroidered, saga-boy shirt and held it up to the light. It was stained with blood. The bull-pistle is the deadliest of all whips. It is made from the penis of a bull that is stretched, cured, and seasoned. Soaked in water and used as a whip, it can momentarily paralyze the strongest adult, sending electric shocks through his body and biting into the skin like fangs. The stranger, at the sight of his blood, and with the white rum making his head spin, broke down and sobbed. Uncle B., in the midst of despising the powder-puff man from the city, felt sorry for him. He took a big red bandanna out of his hip pocket and soaking it in rum, walked over and said gently, "Hold on, pardner, this will sting." He dabbed the blood from the two wounds that reached from victim's shoulders to his waist, forming a perfect X. It was as if Chantal had left a signature on the stranger's soft effeminate back. The wounded man ground his teeth, and sweat rolled down his brow, mingling with his tears. Amagan fetched a packet of coarse salt. But when Uncle B. applied it to the cleaned wounds, the stranger fainted dead away.

Chantal was still facing the door, as he waited for Beltina to join him. The women made way for her and she emerged from their midst. She had a prospecting knife in her right hand, and approaching Chantal, she struck him on the side of his head with the flat part of the long blade. In the forest, that was known as planasting. He fell to the floor and was out like a light.

She flung the prospecting knife down beside him, stepped over the inert body, faced the astonished males, and said, "All-yuh, look after him. Ah didn't kill him, ah jus' sting him a bit. Time an' again I was warning him that the next time he raised his hand against me, or ordered me around in front of my friends, that would be the end of us as man and wife, but the blasted man has hard ears. From now on, I'm not Chantal's woman or any man's woman, I'm my own sweet self, my own woman! Me, and me alone, will decide who I go out with, and when!"

The men were dumbfounded, speechless, but the whores stamped their feet to emphasize their solidarity and approval.

"Good night, Beltina-gal, walk good!" they sang out, following her out of the shop.

They waited until Beltina drove off in the family Land Rover and then they returned to the shop to deal with Chantal and the man from Georgetown. Toad, reaching into the warm valley between her breasts, brought out a bottle of smelling salts and Marabunta Lucy, opening it, moved it back and forth under the two unconscious men's nostrils until they stirred and opened their eyes.

"Is all right, pardners," the women reassured them, as they helped them to their feet, and when they couldn't stand, they carried them to their beds at the back of the shop. While the two were still in a daze and only half-conscious, they heard peels of bawdy laughter coming from the women as they fired one for the road.

HUNTERS AND HUNTED

OLD MAN DOORNE AND HIS TWO ELDER SONS walked through the swamp with the ease of men who had known the feel of mud and water all their lives. But Tonic, the youngest, splashed and stumbled every now and then. The afternoon sun, fierce and yellowing, flung shadows behind them long as fallen coconut palms. The old man was carrying a wareshi. His back was arched and the harness bit into his forehead and shoulders.

Ahead of them was Black Bush, a belt of virgin rain forest that rolled inland like a green ocean. Leading into Black Bush was a sandy plain which the tropical sun had calcined and the wind swept clean of undergrowth except for a few clumps of razor grass, black sage, and stunted cromanty trees. This was interspersed with golden, sandy reefs and stretches of swamp covered with lotus lilies and water hyacinths.

They crossed a reed bed in the swamp where bisi-bisi and wild cane had jostled the lotus lilies and water hyacinths out of the way.

"Is how much farther we got to go?" Tonic asked plaintively.

"Don't ask stupid question, boy, save you breath for the walk," Doorne said.

"Nobody didn't beg you to come, so why you crying out with strain now? You, self, say you want to hunt. If you want to play man-game, then you got to take man-punishment," Caya, the eldest, said. His brother's whining angered him. It reminded him of his own tiredness.

"Ah! Lef' him alone! The boy young and this swamp got teeth enough to bite the marrow of you bone out of you," Tengar growled from deep inside his belly, and he added gently, "If you get too fatigue, boy, I will carry you over the last stretch."

"No!" old man Doorne shouted. "Let the boy walk it on he own. I don't want no rice-pap mother's boy growing up under mi roof." And he turned around, tilted his head, and glared up at his second son, who towered over him like a giant mora tree over a gnarled and stunted lignum vitae.

The rise and fall of their voices and the plop-plop of their feet sounded unreal in the silence. Far to their right, tall whooping cranes were grazing near a cluster of Victoria Regina lilies that looked like enormous dishes spread out for a banquet of giants. The birds stretched long elegant necks to gaze at the intruders. A flock of ducks and herons bright as flames rose noisily from the bisi-bisi reeds ahead of them. But the cranes stood moving their heads from side. to side nervously and preening their wings for flight. The distant horizon behind those stately birds was a wide stretch fragmented by heat hazes in which mirages appeared and disappeared like phantom black-and-white images on a screen.

As the old man and his sons drew closer to Black Bush they headed for a green narthex that other hunters had created as an entrance to the cool perpetual twilight under the forest canopy. Massed tree trunks, growths of bamboo, and closely woven tapestries of vines and creepers invited them to leave the swamp and set foot on dry land. And this put Doorne in a good mood. He had cut out this narthex himself on his last trip. Huge yellow and blue butterflies danced in shafts of sunlight. Against the dark background their wings were incandescent.

"Come on, Tonic, only lil way to go now, boy. Brace yourself against the mud, keep you foot wide apart to fight it," Doorne said.

"Is how much farther we got to go?" Tonic asked again and his voice was listless like a man with fever.

"Don't worry, small-boy, I will carry you over the las' stretch," Tengar said, stopping to hoist his brother onto his broad back.

"Lef' the boy alone, Tengar!" the old man said fiercely. "He got to learn to be a hunter. Even if he bright like moonlight on still water, is time he understand he can't live by book-learning alone. He too black and ugly to be a book man."

"The boy is you son, old man, but he is mi brother," Tengar said.

Tonic, his legs round Tengar's waist and his hands locked around his neck, looked like a black spider clinging to a tree trunk.

"Put the boy down!" Doorne insisted, blocking Tengar's path.

"Move out the way, old man, and stop making gar-bar," Tengar said, good-naturedly.

"Put the boy down!" Doorne shouted, slipping his prospecting knife out of its leather sheath.

"Old man, don't look for trouble, because when you searching for it tha's the time it does ambush you. Don't bank on mi vexation jus' staying in mi belly and rupturing me, jus' because we is the same flesh and blood."

Caya stepped between them and said, "All you two making mirth or what? Look, stop this fool-acting. Old man, you better put your knife away. If the small-boy too weak to bear the strain is you fault. You encourage he to full-up he head with white-man book and all of we does boast how he going to turn doctor or lawyer. Is you spoil him, not me and Tengar. So ease up on the boy-chile, nuh!"

Growling and muttering, Doorne sheathed his prospecting knife and Tengar moved on.

"Thank you, brother Tengar," Tonic whispered, and the black giant grinned, showing white teeth between well-fleshed lips.

Doorne's face looked like a sky threatening rain. He thrust his head forward and strode on.

A hundred yards from dry land, Caya burst out singing:

> "Kaloo, kaloo,
> Lef' mi echo in the bush las' time.
> Was sundown when wind steal that echo of mine.
> Kaloo, kaloo,
> Sundown wind steal mi echo.
> And I tell Wind leggo mi echo! Leggo!
> But wind wouldn't set mi echo free.
> Wind hide mi echo in the bowels of a tree.
> Wind wouldn't set mi echo free.
> Kaloo, kaloo.
> A who-you bird set mi echo free.
> A who-you bird steal it from the tree.
> Kaloo, kaloo."

Caya sang with a deep bass voice, and because this was their way of celebrating another victory over the swamps, the others joined in the chorus:

"A who-you bird set mi echo free.
A who-you bird steal it from the tree.
Kaloo, kaloo."

Tengar made Tonic walk the last fifty yards and Doorne, although he pretended not to notice, understood that this was done to placate him. The gesture, however, irritated the old man.

"Eh, eh, you get so weak you can't carry you fly-weight brother couple yards," he jeered.

Tengar did not answer his father. Other people's malice was something he could never understand; that it should linger and rankle always baffled him. He was glad that he had his mother's sunny disposition and not his father's brooding and vindictive one.

Tonic staggered across the last stretch of water, and as he forced his way through bisi-bisi and wild cane reeds, they tossed their tasseled heads as if a storm had hit them. Looking at his brother, Caya burst out laughing.

"Go long, Tonic, go long. Go long, mother's boy," he said.

"Ah, leave the small-boy alone," Tengar said.

"Papa Tengar and he boy-child," Doorne taunted.

Tonic crawled up on dry land and lay down, his feet still trailing in the swamp.

"But is why I come on this brute-walk?" he sobbed.

"We tell you wasn't fun; this swamp got teeth, boy," Caya said.

"You only full of 'I tell you this' and 'I tell you that,' but how was I to know that this sun was so hot, that this swamp would be mi kinnah?"

"All right, boy, all right. You hold out well enough," Doorne said, lifting him up and depositing him on higher ground.

Against the whiteness of Tonic's eyeballs the brown irises were luminous. His face had the dark sheen of an otter's pelt, but his lips were powdered with tiny crystals of perspiration.

"Drink this!" Doorne ordered, holding a flask of bush rum to his lips. Tonic swallowed a mouthful and sat up coughing and spitting.

"It hot like fire," he said, opening his mouth wide and gasping.

"Nothing like it to pick you up," Doorne said, taking a swig and passing the flask to Caya and Tengar.

"This is bush-rum-father," Caya said, smacking his lips appreciatively and taking another swig.

"Is Chinaman the old man does get it from," Tengar said looking sideways at his father. Tonic lay still and shut his eyes, but the sun pricked his eyeballs and he turned over on his stomach. The others sat near him with their backs to the sun. Doorne took out a delicately wrought white clay pipe and used a dry stem of para-grass to clean it.

"We really take long to reach Black Bush this time," Caya said.

"All right, don't make bad worse," Tengar said. Tonic had fallen asleep and was wheezing softly. Saliva was running from the corner of his open mouth. The old man struck a match and puffed away at his pipe. In the afternoon sun his head looked like a beach strewn with patches of foam. His face was shaped like an upturned pear, with high Mongolian cheekbones and hollow cheeks tapering down to a pointed cleft chin. It was lean as a harpy eagle's, and his deep-set eyes were restless. Veins stood out like bush rope at the side of his temples, and Tengar could see them throbbing. Ever since he could remember, his father had had those bulging veins at the side of his head. They were barometers that gauged his moods. When Tengar was a boy, he used to think that the old man had lizards puffing under his skin.

"We better start fixing up camp before a tiger snatch-up one of we tonight," Doorne said.

"Rest you bones, old man, long time yet before sundown," Caya said. He sat cross-legged, scratching his naked belly and chewing a black sage stem. His almond-shaped eyes were smoky, slanted, and slightly incongruous in a Negro face. Doorne's sons were all by different mothers, and Caya's had been half-Chinese and half-Negro.

"Come on, get up!" Doorne ordered, and he turned on Caya. "What I forget 'bout this part of the world you en't begin to learn yet. Who is you, boy, to tell you father 'bout when is time to pitch camp?"

"All right, old man, all right. Stop frying-up you lil fat," Caya said standing up and stretching.

Tonic was rested and refreshed, and he went to the edge of the forest to gather firewood. The afternoon sun had lost its sting, and flocks of birds were flying home after feeding in the swamps or on the seashore. Parrots screamed and chattered in the nearby trees as Tonic hacked at dry branches with his cutlass. A snake with silvery scales slithered past him and he chopped it in two, watching the halves wriggle until his father bellowed at him to hurry up. Tengar and Caya had already driven uprights into the soft ground and were tying on crossbeams with liana vines.

"Go and bring some troolie palm leaf, boy, and do it bird-speed!" Caya ordered. Tonic obeyed quickly. He didn't want darkness to catch him too far away from the others. He heard the night wind in the trees and shivered.

Night fell suddenly. The lazy mosquitoes that had been sleeping under the trees all day came out in clouds. The old man and his sons crouched around the fire, bathing their limbs in smoke. As soon as a tongue of flame escaped they smothered it with green branches and leaves. Doorne left his sons and sat away from the fire. He heard Tonic alternately coughing from the smoke and slapping mosquitoes.

"You can't control yourself, boy?" he shouted.

"These mosquitoes stinging like pepper, Papa."

"Damn balls!"

"Your blood get old and bitter, old man, mosquito don't like it nomore," Caya said.

"Don't make you eyes pass me, boy," the old man said chuckling.

"They going to let up in a lil while, I can feel the wind clearing up the thickness in the air," Tengar said encouragingly. He inhaled the aromatic smell of wild mango in the wood smoke and remembered how his mother used to burn green limbs inside their hut to kill the stink of dirty bedclothes and sweat.

Dew fell noiselessly and the night wind grew chill. A piper owl sang to the new moon.

"They say them owl is jumbie bird, and nobody never see one," Tonic said hugging his knees.

"I see plenty. They got big eye and they does eat small snake," Tengar said.

"When I was young I try to tame one, jus' to hear he sing when the moon come out, but the one I had never sing a note and he kill so much of the neighbor chicken that mi mother drown he in a bucket of water," Doorne said.

They ate tasso and cassava bread for dinner, and when Tonic complained that the tasso was like a car tire, Doorne boasted, "I chewing up this tasso like it is fresh meat," and he added, spitting out a splinter of bone, "All you young boy teeth mek out of jelly or what?"

The fire burned steadily and the green logs hissed. In the firelight, Doorne's face could have been a burnished mask nailed against the wall of darkness.

Tengar, Caya, and Tonic lay in their hammocks. Tonic had fallen asleep instantly, but his brothers watched the stars through holes in the thatch. They heard the piper owl fluting its melodies to the moon, a tinamou singing across the treetops to its mate, howler baboons roaring, and the wind in the bamboo trees. The sounds faded and died in sleep.

A family of red howlers feeding on bamboo shoots woke them up at daybreak. Doorne brought the dying fire to a blaze while his three sons went down to the edge of the swamp to bathe. They sat down to a breakfast of turtle eggs, salted fish, biscuits, and unleavened bread with bits of pork in it, and they washed the meal down with tea.

"I had a funny dream last night," Tonic said, putting a whole turtle egg into his mouth. He always spoke quickly. His mind seemed to push his words out before tongue and lips had time to form them. "I dream that a lot of tigers were coughing across the river."

"Was that tasso sitting heavy on you stomach, boy?" Doorne said, and wiping his mouth on his sleeve, he added, "We got to get going."

"But that wasn't all the dream," Tonic said.

"Well, tell it quick. We got to go," Doorne said.

"There was an old black man on the other side of the canal and he had teeth like a shark, and every time he talk or sing he teeth was so sharp that they cut his tongue and he mouth was always dripping blood," Tonic said.

"Blood is a good thing to dream 'bout, boy. It mean that one of we going to make some money," Caya said.

They set out immediately after the meal. There was no washing up as they had used waterlily leaves for dishes. Doorne led the way into the twilight of Black Bush. Once out of reach of the sun's rays there was no undergrowth, and they moved swiftly, silently across a carpet of rotting leaves. Crouching slightly forward, the old man almost merged with his surroundings. He and Tengar had the hunter's ability to become more shadow than substance in the forest. Doorne noticed every movement, even the wind stirring in the leaves high above him. A green parrot snake slid down a mora tree in front of them, and when Tonic pointed at it excitedly, his father signaled at him to be quiet. The snake disappeared in the underbush. A bush rabbit stopped in the middle of the trail, standing on its hind legs and examining them with quick darting glances. It sensed no danger. The parrot snake struck so swiftly that the watchers heard a cry and only then noticed that the snake had coiled around the rabbit. Doorne whispered to his sons, and they walked on quickly until he picked up the trail of a herd of wild hogs. He knelt down and examined the cloven hoof-prints carefully.

"They been passing by here couple days well," Doorne whispered. He followed the trail for a little distance, stopped, and picked up a section of a snake's backbone.

"Them hog kill a big snake here. That parrot snake better watch out. Once he swallow the rabbit he can't move too far," the old man said in an undertone. He knelt down on the trail again. "This is tiger footmark here, fresh footmark. Is a big puss. He must be following the hog for a meal." His eyes scanned the trees. "Let we climb up on this one and wait."

Doorne led the way to a big tree with branches spreading over the trail. He wedged his wareshi between two branches. The others followed him, and they built a rough platform and settled down to wait. Tonic was fidgety, but his father and brothers sat alert and still. They were about twenty feet up, and above them the tree grew over a hundred feet, boring through the forest ceiling to reach the sunlight. Tonic wormed his way from one end of the platform to the other, and Doorne clapped a hand on his boy shoulder.

"Stay quiet!" he hissed. "If you go too near the edge and fall out even Jesus' weeping wouldn't help you."

"I hearing something," Tengar said and a moment later he pointed down the trail. A fully-grown Maipuri jaguar, walking noiselessly on padded feet merged with the sunlight and shadows dappling the forest floor. A male marudi bird sounded raucous alarms, and a female responded from deep inside the forest. There were green fires in the jaguar's eyes as he sniffed suspiciously. He seemed to have picked up their scent, although they were downwind. Tonic imagined that the jaguar's eyes and his own were making four all the time. Doorne loaded his fifteen-bore shotgun and waited. Tengar and Caya did not move. They trusted the old man's marksmanship.

The thunder of wild hogs coming down the trail broke the silence. The jaguar turned round and sprang onto a branch hanging over the trail not far from the other four watchers.

"We going to have some sport, today," Doorne said, and his sons laughed mirthlessly, never taking their eyes off the jaguar.

The leader of the herd appeared, then the flock, moving in a tightly packed phalanx with the sows and their young ones bringing up the rear. The earth shook with hoofbeats, the forest vibrated with atavistic grunts, and the smell of musk was almost overpowering. Tonic clung to Tengar; the feel of his brother's warm, muscular body was reassuring.

The jaguar waited until the main body of hogs had passed by and there were only about a dozen stragglers. He pounced on a fat sow and buried curved fangs into its neck. There was a piercing squeal cut short by a gurgle. The rest of the flock turned around and stampeded toward the attacker. When the jaguar sprang back on the tree, with the hog still gripped in his jaws, the branch broke under the extra weight and the jaguar fell in the midst of the flock. He released the dead hog and snarled, certain of his strength. As the milling, grunting pack closed in, he forced his way through with fangs and fury, maddened by the scent of blood. The hogs that could not reach their enemy turned on the wounded and dying of their own kind. Four times, it seemed as if the jaguar had cleared enough space around him to spring free, but each time the maddened herd surged in again. The spot on which the big cat fought became a whirlpool in the middle of a stream of hogs.

"He done kill 'bout twenty of them," Doorne said, but the others did not hear him.

The jaguar went down twice more, but he came up and fought back in a frenzy of ebbing strength. He snarled a hoarse admission of defeat and went down for the last time. The hogs played tug-o'-war with his intestines and when nothing was left but bloodstained skin and bones, they remained milling around uncertainly.

Whenever Tonic looked away from the scene of the carnage, his eyes fell on the shotgun across Tengar's knees. He had been allowed to use it a few times, but Tengar always complained that cartridges were expensive, and that a shotgun was not a small-boy's toy.

"Let me take a shot, Tengar," he pleaded, but his brother either did not hear him or ignored him. Tonic felt that this was a good chance to bag one or even two of the hogs. He would be a hero at school if he did. He looked at Tengar and then at the gun. He reached for the gun and no one seemed to notice when he raised the stock to his shoulder and fired quickly. He did not bother to aim or hold the gun close. The recoil flung him backwards and before Tengar could reach out to save him, he fell from the platform. The twenty-foot drop dazed him and he sat in the midst of the hogs, showing the whites of his frightened eyes. The gun lay beside him with one barrel still loaded, but he made no attempt to pick it up.

The hogs closed in and he screamed. Fear gave him strength and cunning. He ran toward the base of the tree. If he reached it he could climb up a liana. The flock came after him. Tengar stamped his feet and shouted, trying to draw their attention. Then, he sprang down from the platform, a prospecting knife in one hand and a cutlass in the other. Most of the hogs followed Tonic, but Tengar stamped his feet again and shouted, still trying to call them away. Tonic, running deer-speed, sprang on to a thick liana, but it had too much slack and he dropped back. He saw the hogs baring their teeth below him and tugged frantically at the vine. Tengar fought the hogs off by crouching low and hacking at their legs. Doorne and Caya sat on the platform, looking on helplessly, the old man fingering the trigger of his gun, and Caya shouting encouragement.

"Hold on, Tonic! Climb up, boy! Don't frighten, small-boy!"

A big hog caught Tonic by the heel and hauled him down. Tengar had cleared a way to within ten feet of his brother.

"I coming, Tonic, I coming, boy!" he called out, sweat glistening on his limbs. Tengar's strength was greater because he was unconscious of it. It was something vibrating in his body like anger or laughter. Many of the hogs had turned away from Tonic and were attacking him now. Every time they rushed at him, he swung his cutlass, chopping off forelegs like twigs. Tonic was screaming and foam whitened his lips. Before Tengar reached him, the boy's legs suddenly seemed to melt; he grew shorter and shorter. His screams subsided into a rhythmic moaning.

When Tengar cleared a path to his brother, all that was left of the boy's legs were frayed stumps gushing blood and protruding bones with jagged ends. Doorne and Caya joined them. The old man went down on one knee and fired into the flock until the barrel of his gun was too hot to touch. The hogs, their leaders dead, turned and ran.

Tonic was lying face down with one eye pressed against a big, star-shaped leaf stained with drops of blood. Ants were scurrying up and down the leaf, and before lapsing into unconsciousness, he saw them as huge monsters. Doorne tied a tourniquet around the stumps, cooing to his son all the time like a mother baboon nursing a wounded baby. The sweet and sickly smell of blood and death was everywhere. Caya helped his father wash Tonic's wounds, but Tengar stood with his back against the tree holding the dripping cutlass in his hand. A sense of community was awakened between Doorne and his sons. He was again the father, the one in authority.

"You got some water in you balata pouch? Give the boy some and wash this froth off his mouth," he ordered and Tengar obeyed mechanically. Caya went around clubbing wounded hogs to death. The ground was slippery. Tengar wet his handkerchief and mopped his brother's face. Tonic opened his eyes and shock, pain, and loss of blood made him speak in whispers.

"Tengar, me don't want Mantop to call me yet but I feeling funny. Mi head feel like a kite flying in the wind."

"Don't talk so much, boy. Lie down quiet," Doorne said.

"Is why mi foot feelin' so heavy, Papa?"

"You get injure, boy, them hog injure you bad."

"Tengar!"

"Aye, aye, small-boy."

"Is how you does know when Mantop come for you?"

"You does jus' know, small-boy. You don't never need no prophet to tell you."

"Is how you does know...how you does know...how...?" Tonic's voice trailed off. Tengar and Doorne stood over him crying softly. The skin around the stumps of Tonic's legs was turning yellow.

"You think he got a chance?" Caya asked.

"He loss too much blood," Doorne, said. Each breath that Tonic took sounded as if it was retching its way out of his body. Suddenly, the breathing stopped, and blood poured from his mouth.

"Small-boy! Small-boy!" Tengar called urgently. Tonic's eyes looked like eggs in a dark nest.

Caya was calculating how much money the pork would fetch in the village. He did not notice when his brother died. Tengar covered the dead boy's legs with a dirty blanket and stood over the corpse.

"Is why folks like we does die so stupid!" he shouted, waving his arms about, challenging invisible phantoms whom he was sure lurked everywhere under the listening trees. "Is why we folks does die so stupid? In other places, they say, people does die for something worthwhile. But is why Tonic die, tell me that?"

BRA ANANCY AND TIGER

Bra Anancy, the spider-man, is a character in West African folklore, and the slaves, uprooted from Africa and brought to the West Indies, made him the central figure in numerous folk tales. African folklore depicted him as a man of the forest, and a keeper of the rainbow, but in his West-Indianized form, he moved from the forest to the city, becoming a likeable rogue, a smart-man, and a trickster. Those slaves who were uprooted from their African homeland, and who, after emancipation, became the peasants of the Caribbean, made Anancy the symbol of their wish-fulfillment. This trickster spider-man was always able to outwit the rich and powerful. In the imaginations of those who were constantly hard-pressed and threatened with destitution, Anancy was the archetypal survivor. They saw him as a clever Lotus Eater who was always able to enjoy the good things of life without brutalizing his body with hard work.

BRA ANANCY WAS A SWEET-SKINNED MAN, and the old ones used to say that when laziness was sharing, he grabbed more than his fair share. Just as how Bra Anancy could live in lazy ease through the nights and days, his neighbor Tiger was the hardest working Busha-landowner for miles around. From foreday morning to can't-see-time, Tiger walked about softly-softly planting corn, ground nuts, cassava, rice, sweet potatoes, and yams. Besides, coconut palms and a variety of fruit trees grew along the outer edges of his land. To see Tiger's farm when his crops were ripening and his fruit orchards were alive with birds would have pleased anybody's heart. But, while Tiger was watering the land with the sweat of his brow, Bra Anancy would lazy-away the hours in a hammock that he strung in the shade of a mango tree. Days would slip by while he lay there thinking up schemes of how to sweet-talk Tiger into sharing the fruits of his labor.

One morning when Bra Anancy was dallying away the hours in his hammock as usual, humming popular tunes, and reaching up every now and then to pick a ripe mango, Tiger crept up on him silently and greeted him in a loud voice that almost made him jump out of his skin.

"Morning, neighbor!"

"Man, I always told you not to creep up on me like that!"

"Creep up on you? Walking softly is something that I do all the time."

Bra Anancy, shifting his body into a more comfortable position, yawned and said, "Anyway, Tiger. What good wind blows you this way so early in the morning?"

"Early in the morning? It's nearly lunchtime!"

A fly settled on the tip of Bra Anancy's nose, but he was too lazy to brush it away, so he let it crawl across his forehead.

"I came to collect the rent, neighbor," Tiger said.

"But, Tiger, man, why are you harassing me so? If I told you once, I told you a dozen times that as soon as the big deal I'm working on comes off, I'll pay you the rent with interest."

Tiger scratched the side of his face thoughtfully, and this made his long whiskers tremble, but Bra Anancy, pretending to be very annoyed, turned in his hammock and showed Tiger his back.

"Tiger," he grumbled, "I'm a man of my word, and you're my best friend. If you don't trust me, then who will, my brother? You're treating your best friend like an outcast. Besides," Bra Anancy said, turning to face Tiger once more and speaking confidentially, "I promised to take you to the fair, remember? And—"

"Oh, yes, Bra Anancy. The fair!" Tiger interrupted him, and continued eagerly, "You said the prettiest girls in the whole district will be there, man, and you promised to introduce me to a Beauty Queen and her three sisters."

"One sister," Bra Anancy corrected him.

"OK, one sister."

"Looks like I wouldn't be able to take you to that fair after all, Tiger. This rent business is causing me plenty worries and with it weighing on my mind I'm sure I won't be able to have a good bacchanal. Perhaps we can go to the fair the next time it comes around to these parts—"

"No, no, Bra Anancy, don't say that, man," Tiger begged. "I'll wait for the rent until your big deal comes off."

Tiger lived in a big house on the hill, and from the top of the hill, all the land you could see from his doorstep to the rim of the horizon belonged to him. Tiger was always dressed-to-kill in fancy striped clothes, and he was a handsome backra-man to look at. But even with all this, when it came to sweet-talking women, Bra Anancy could run rings around him.

Although, to tell you the truth, Bra Anancy had a very difficult beauty. The first time his own mother set eyes on him, she said that any child as ugly as the one she just gave birth to needed to have more luck than there were shells on the seashore. And, indeed, Bra Anancy was born with plenty of luck, because in spite of his off-putting looks and the way he had of walking as if he had two left arms and two right legs, he had managed to sail through life eating and drinking well, sweet-talking the finest of women into going out with him, and always having a decent place to live.

All of this was achieved by Anancy while he remained a steadfast stranger to hard work. When you looked at Bra Anancy closely, you could see that his skin had the dark sheen of a ripe star apple, he had bulging eyes of a tarzia, and when he laughed his big-belly laugh, his teeth were white as tiger orchids and his whole body enjoyed the burst of mirth. Besides, even though his limbs didn't seem to hang right on his body, he had the swagger of a sweet-man who believed that he was God's gift to women. The truth of the matter was that Bra Anancy knew only too well that the prettier the woman, the more awkward and tongued-tied a suitor became when he pitched a saga-boy line at her. So his bold-as-brass approach, and his laughing, easygoing manner was a change from the clumsy passes made by country bumpkins.

Tiger went back to work thinking about the beautiful women he would meet at the fair, and smiling to himself every now and then.

After all, he told himself, I can afford to pay more bride-money than anyone in these parts, and when good looks were sharing, I got more than my fair share.

Bra Anancy lay back in his hammock and began to daydream about how he was going to spend Tiger's money and have a rip-roaring bacchanal at the fair. The daydream was so vivid that it made him hungry, so he helped himself to ripe mangoes, sugar apples, papayas, and a juicy pineapple from Tiger's farm. After peeling and feasting on them, he buried the skins and seeds and returned to his hammock for a siesta. He hummed a popular Calypso tune, scratched his belly contentedly, and soon fell fast asleep. And when a cow fly stung him, he woke up momentarily, swatted it, and promptly went back to sleep.

On the day of the fair, Tiger woke up at the crack of dawn and hurrying over to Bra Anancy's house, called out, "Wake up, Bra Anancy; we've got a big day ahead of us!"

"Oh, it's you, Tiger! Man, you're acting like a bushman going to town for the first time—a never-see-come-to-see!"

A reluctant Bra Anancy climbed out of his hammock, picked a black sage stem, chewed and softened the end of it, and then used it to clean his teeth. Tiger, looking on impatiently, played with his long whiskers and tapped the ground with his right forepaw.

"For heaven's sake, hurry up Bra Anancy!"

"Keep a cool head, Tiger; the sun's barely nudging itself above the treetops; mists are still clinging to the trees and the green pastures."

"But Bra Anancy, you haven't even started to get dressed yet, man."

"Get dressed, Tiger?"

"Yes."

"These clothes I've slept in are the very ones I'm planning to wear."

"But your shirt and slacks are filled with more holes than a honeycomb."

"Exactly."

"Man, you must be making jokes!"

"No, Tiger, this is all the dress I'm dressing."

Tiger smiled to himself because he felt that for once he could have the edge on Bra Anancy when they met the pretty women at the fair.

With my fancy striped clothes and soft-soled shoes, the women will only have eyes for me, he told himself.

It was a long walk to the fair, and Bra Anancy, much to Tiger's annoyance, made frequent rest stops. A roof of treetops kept the sun out, and it was cool and dark in the forest. Tiger walked silently under the canopy, but you could hear Bra Anancy's feet crushing dead leaves and popping twigs as he sauntered along. They came to a stretch of soft, white sand, and Bra Anancy stopped to pick a wild pineapple. He peeled it with his hunting knife and ate it with such relish that the juice spilled out of his mouth, ran down his neck, and onto his chest.

"Have a piece, Tiger. Man, this is the sweetest pineapple I've tasted for a long time."

"No, thank you, Bra Anancy. I don't want to risk staining my clothes with pineapple juice," Tiger said smugly.

They continued in silence until Bra Anancy blurted out, "Tiger, you really and truly look as if you own earth and sky."

Tiger adjusted his bow tie and showed all of his teeth in a big, satisfied grin. "If you only knew how far I had to go to get this outfit. And it cost me plenty," Tiger declared proudly.

But Bra Anancy looked very thoughtful for a while, and then he said gravely, "You know, Tiger, it just occurred to me that the Beauty Queen and her sister don't like rich folk who make a big show of their wealth. They have so many suitors following them like dogs in heat that they can pick and choose who they want to go out with. They're the kind of women who tend to judge a man more by his manners and his brains than by something as ordinary as what he's wearing. I've seen them turn down a rich, dressed-to-kill man for a fellow who was casually dressed but well-spoken."

"But, Bra Anancy, you're a wicked man, eh! Why didn't you tell me this before we left home? You know I'm not the kind of man who makes a big fuss about clothes," Tiger lied.

"Well, what I would suggest at this late stage is this," Bra Anancy said, acting as if he was about to do Tiger a great favor. "Since I know the young women already, perhaps we can exchange clothes—you wear my modest shirt and trousers, and I'll put on your fancy striped suit."

"But, Bra Anancy, man—" Tiger began to protest. Bra Anancy, however, cut him short. "Do you want to make a good impression on the Beauty Queen and her sister or not?"

"Well, if like you say, they're smart and beautiful as the mystery of sleep, yes, I definitely want to meet them."

Without further argument, they went into the bushes by the roadside and changed clothes. When they emerged, Bra Anancy looked like a prince while Tiger looked like a beggar.

"I hope you're right," Tiger said, feeling uncomfortable in Bra Anancy's sweaty clothes.

"You'll soon see that I did the right thing, pardner," Bra Anancy assured him.

But as soon as they reached the fairground Bra Anancy began to strut and give himself airs, until everyone thought Bra Anancy was Tiger's Lord and Master.

"Why are you acting so bosey? And where's this Beauty Queen and her sister you promised to introduce me to?" the irate Tiger asked.

"Patience, Tiger! Have patience, man!"

Tiger growled under his breath and held back the sharp response that was at the tip of his tongue. The drummers were practicing their start-up rhythms, and the bongo players were warming up the goatskin on their ornate drums. Flutes, panpipes, charangos, and guitars were harmonizing their tunes until they sounded like a large orchestra. Food and drinks were passed around freely. The Apinti drummers' chanted voices and the bongo accompaniment went to Anancy's head like rum. He began to dance like a man possessed.

Tiger dragged him aside in between dances and said angrily, "Look at how you're sweating-up my new clothes! You'd better find that Beauty Queen and her sisters right now or I'll head for home."

"Ah told you before, Tiger, it's one sister."

"All right the Beauty Queen and one sister, and don't think for one moment I'll leave you to sport around in my Sunday-best clothes! When I go the outfit goes with me."

Bra Anancy saw that Tiger's eyes were turning yellow with vexation, and he knew that he had to do something to placate him. So he led the way through the crowd of revelers until he came to a platform where the Beauty Queen and her sister were seated. Although the two women couldn't remember having ever set eyes on Bra Anancy before, he greeted them with an easy familiarity, saying, "I'm glad to see you again, ladies. And you know what?" They smiled and he continued, "You're even more beautiful than when I saw you last, and I didn't think that was possible. You make birds of paradise look ugly and, by the way, this is my friend Tiger."

The women glanced at Tiger, and immediately looking away from him had eyes for only the cunning Bra Anancy.

Tiger, in the meantime, forgot his vexation and was feasting his eyes on the two ladies so that if you slapped him on the back, his eyes would've popped out.

One sister's name was Sota, and the other one, Rena, and both of them were as pretty as lady's-slipper orchids. Bra Anancy, moving closer to them, began swapping friendly banter until he sounded like a songbird warbling in the mating season. But the more they seemed to be enjoying one another's company, the more alone and neglected Tiger felt.

When it was time to head for home, Anancy invited the beauty queens to be his guests.

"I live in a big house on a hilltop and have servants who will take care of your every need," he said, and then lowering his voice, he promised to dress them up in silk and satin finery and jewelry galore.

Tiger, with ugly thoughts knocking together inside his head, called Bra Anancy aside and growled, "I thought you told me those gals didn't like rich people."

"Sshhh!" Bra Anancy cautioned, "You want to mash up the whole scheme, man?"

But Tiger was still angry, and he said, "I think it's time we changed clothes, Bra Anancy."

Sota and Rena noticing the mounting tension between Anancy and his friend began getting restive, but Bra Anancy's lively outpouring of small talk continued to amuse them.

Tiger decided to wait a little longer. "Wait till we reach home. I'm going to see if Mr. Anancy will have the barefacedness to take these two sisters to his smell-up hut," he mused and he could hardly hold back the laughter while he was walking behind them.

Night caught them on the trail, and when the waracabra birds began to chatter and the red howler baboons started growling like thunder, the two sisters got frightened and said, "Bra Anancy, we want to go home to our papa's house."

And when they looked back and saw Tiger's eyes shining like green fire, they got even more frightened.

"I swear that I will marry Sota, and find the right swain for Rena," Bra Anancy promised. "Soon as foreday-morning breaks, I'm going to send a runner to your papa with the bride-money. So cross my heart and hope to die if everything doesn't turn out like I promise."

Now, there were few things in life that Anancy enjoyed more than the company of pretty women, but he also knew that when the story moves from come-see-me to come-live-with-me, then women need a lot more than sweet-talk. So smart-man Bra Anancy hit on a new scheme.

All of a sudden, he began to laugh until tears were running down his cheeks. When the two girls asked what was the reason for this burst of merriment, he said, "But look how I fooled all you about my friend Tiger!"

"How you mean, Bra Anancy?"

"Just because the man dress-up in old clothes, all you believe that he's some kind of beggar-man." And he lowered his voice and whispered, "The man is really and truly a prince in disguise."

"A prince?"

"Yes, his father was King Tiger, and he put on those ragged clothes only to fool people," Bra Anancy explained.

"I always knew he had some kind of special quality about him," Sota said.

"Didn't I tell you he looked like a proud man?" Rena said.

The two sisters slowed down and began to make a big fuss over Tiger. By the time they reached his big house on the hill, Rena had wrapped herself around him like a flowering vine, while Sota settled down with the sweet-talking Bra Anancy.

Tiger built a special house for Bra Anancy and Sota some distance away from his own mansion. And to this day, if you happen to pass by his house, you can see Tiger, the two sisters, and several children working in the fields while Bra Anancy is stretched in his hammock on the veranda, scratching his ample belly and dozing peacefully.

THE INITIATION OF BELFON

Carib Shamans say that you must
not gaze at the full moon too long
or your head will become muddled
and your body will become a house of dreams.

I SAT IN THE BOW OF THE VICTOR P, and watched the reflection of the full moon on the River. The Victor P, sitting deep in the water with its heavy load of forest products and a full complement of passengers, was being swept along by the running tide. The moon was a magical lure a stone's throw ahead, but the Victor P never caught up with it. I fell asleep and dreamt about plunging into the river and capturing the moon. This was the last stretch of my three-week journey from the hills, mountains, and savannahs of Biaro.

We arrived at the Stabroek Market wharf when the high tide was about to peak and trade winds were stirring up sun-silvered wavelets across wide stretches of the river's estuary. I thanked Captain Rhodius for bringing me safely to my destination. He was a friend of Atlassa, my godfather and guardian, and he interrupted the orders he shouted to the crew of the Victor P to give me some raunchy advice. "Walk well, young Belfon. But remember they have plenty sharks in this city. So keep a padlock on your pockets and a raincoat on your sugar-stick, and never ride a horse without a saddle, it makes your bottom sore."

The other passengers guffawed and laughed out loud, and a market woman declared in a loud and sarcastic voice, "Young man, nobody can give you better advice about whoring in this town than Captain Rhodius! So listen well to what him have to tell you about walking down the road to perdition."

I collected my luggage and making my way through a noisy but good-natured

51

crowd, headed for the square in front of the market. I was wearing a Llanero outfit—a leather vest, a wide-brimmed leather sombrero, leather pants, and riding boots. Beltina, Atlassa's common-law wife, had warned me that I'd have to wear more conventional attire in Trinidad, and she had sent me off with a suitcase full of shirt-jacks, slacks, a couple of linen suits, and four pairs of handmade moccasins. These were all send-off gifts from the folks in Biaro, since I was the first student from that community to have won a place at a university. I was on my way to study Engineering at the St. Augustine campus of the University of the West Indies.

I made my way to the taxi stand in the square in front of the market. A grizzled old fellow, his balding head several inches below my shoulder, walked up to me. "You mus' be Mistah Belfon. Couvade told me to look out for yuh when the riverboat came in. My name is Dalton and they call me Daltee. I'm from Belladrum on the West Coast." The simple and forthright way in which Dalton introduced himself made me feel at ease for the first time since I had disembarked. I believed that by telling me his name, his nickname, and the village in which he was born, he was intimating that like me, he was a roots-man whose umbilical chord was buried under a tree in a village.

"Pleased to meet you, Mr. Dalton." I offered him my hand, but he ignored it.

"I never shake hands," he said calmly. "Jus' pay me the fifteen-dollar fare when we reach Couvade yard," and he didn't utter another word for the rest of the journey. I was surprised by this rebuff, but I wasn't offended, for I still remembered how bad-tempered and insensitive city folk could be.

I loaded my suitcases and the baskets of gifts I had brought for Couvade into sourpuss Daltee's taxi. Atlassa had sent her salted Hymara fish, tasso, dried hearts of awaraballi and troolie palms, balata sculptures, aromatic herbs, strips of amarata bark for lighting fires, and dried flowers that retained their colors and perfumed scent. As we sped along the highway, fresh sea breezes rushing into the van through its open windows made me drowsy, and landscapes passed by in a blur.

The Biaro I just left—Atlassa's Biaro—is a huge Nature Preserve he had leased from the Government. He had lived abroad for decades before returning home to live in this primordial setting. This patriarch of Biaro had rescued me from the Georgetown streets, and apart from trips to the Roraima savannahs of Brazil, I had not left that community of dispossessed Caribs, renegades and castaways from several countries for fourteen years, and for months, in those interludes between sleeping and waking, I'd been daydreaming about what it would be like to be a stranger in a strange land, for everywhere outside of Biaro was a strange land to me.

The taxi turned off at right angles into a village road, and I became fully awake as the bumpy rodeo ride took me past sugarcane fields, dark groves of trees, houses perched on tall stilts, and canals with molasses-colored water that mirrored the sky. When the van came to a stop, it puffed and rattled long after the driver had switched off the ignition.

Couvade's cottage was raised high on greenheart posts with finely woven Amerindian hammocks strung between them. The hammocks looked like webs spun by giant spiders, and the ground under them was covered with a mixture of cow dung and mud spread and smoothed by hand. A footpath meandered its way through wild azaleas, blood-red hibiscus blooms, flowering acacias, and clumps of tall decorative grasses that led to the front steps, where scented mimosa vines clung to the banisters all the way up to the porch. A towering hog plum tree shaded the backyard and littered the ground with bright yellow fruit that attracted bees and butterflies and ants. When I unloaded my luggage and paid Daltee, I thanked him, but he ignored me:

"Ah delivered yuh guest safe and sound," he said, and waving to Couvade, drove away.

"He's a tight-lipped fellow," I said, and Couvade agreed: "Is easier to squeeze water out of stone than to get a few sentences out of Daltee."

The lane down which he disappeared was surfaced with burnt earth, and it wound its way through neat rows of wooden cottages interspersed with mud huts. It had rained earlier in the day and the rutted road looked like a bloodstained bandage.

A tall, slender, and shapely Couvade with black curly hair, enormous dark eyes, and skin as smooth as that of a ripe star apple, greeted me with a voice as clear and sweet as a bellbird's. I had expected to see an old woman and not this ageless beauty.

"Don't worry with Daltee! Come in, boy! But what a way you grow tall and broad and strong like a dakama! Last time I set eyes on you, you were nothing but a long streak of misery—all elbows and knees and white tiger-orchid eyes and a face that didn't beat against enough years to tell if it was a woman-face or a man-face. Watch out for your head, now! This place en't built for men like you and your wicked godfather." She changed the subject abruptly. Her thoughts seemed to be racing ahead of her words. "So, old man Atlassa sent some gifts for me, eh? Well, I must say that he always remembers me when somebody's coming this way from Biaro. He knows how bad the food situation is in this coastland of plenty dogs and few bones."

"Atlassa also sent this letter, Couvade," I said, handing it to her, and putting it in a pocket of her skirt, she said, "Atlassa always writes long epistles, so I'll read this one later." She stood at a window that looked out on a sea of golden-tasseled sugarcane fields, and was lost in thought. The room was sparsely furnished, but a tall outsized bookshelf had been wedged into one corner and the books were arranged so neatly that one suspected that they had not been read recently. On one of the small tables there were black porcelain angels and they faced white devils with pointed, elongated ears and long arrow-headed tails and, on a small veranda ringed with hanging ferns, there were two reclining Berbice chairs. I wondered how Couvade, Ti-Zek, and her five children had managed to fit into this doll's house of theirs.

"But the afternoon hot, eh! Let me make some lemonade for you, boy," Couvade said.

"How is Ti-Zek?" I asked. "He hasn't come our way in Biaro for some time."

"Gold fever's got him by the balls again. Last word I had from him, he was near Apoteri on the edge of the Rupununi savannah; and as for mi five children, not one of them's with me as you can see. So you come at a good time, Belfon, because this house is as empty as a sky without sun and moon and stars."

As she walked away to prepare the lemonade, my eyes traced the contours of her body in her pale blue dress. I tried to avert my gaze, but couldn't. She served me a citrus drink sweetened with brown sugar and flavored with nutmeg and Demerara rum. I drank it from a large enamel cup. There was an impish smile on her face when she asked:

"How old are you, young brigah-man?"

"I was twenty last month," I said.

"What a thing it is to be twenty, boy! You can conquer earth and sky but you won't know how to do it till you get too old and tired even to try."

"I'm going to the university to study engineering," I said, making conversation to cover up my uneasiness.

"In Jamaica?" she enquired.

"No, Trinidad. Without my godfather Atlassa, I could never have done it."

"Atlassa and Father Marquez, birds of a feather! The big chibat from Biaro and the Jesuit priest! One rescued you from streets that were your kinnah, and the other scooped me up from a mud hut in a village. Them two met in the Biara hills and became tight as goatskin to a drum. The one turn you into a book-learning man, and the other turn me into a preacher-woman. The two of them were what Matawa the Carib Chief called sleepers of the dreamtime. All I know is the two dreamed the same blasted dream. When I was growing up, I don't think a day passed without Atlassa or Beltina bringing up Father Marquez's name. When that priest disappeared Atlassa grieved for him something awful."

Couvade's eyes wandered away into distances far beyond the landscape outside her window. She continued talking, and it was as though my presence had induced her to unload a stream of reminiscences:

"I wish I had enough book-learning to take a walk inside Atlassa's head because he and Father Marquez misshaped my life, and then left me. Plenty of times I heard Atlassa quarreling with Beltina, telling her she should read some book or the other; and listening, I knew that he was talking to me, too." Couvade, sitting carelessly in the Berbice chair, framed her beautiful face with two hands and continued:

"Father Marquez used to pour all kinds of vexation on my young head. He wanted me to read every book he suggested. But Beltina and me, we're not book-people, instead, we're sisters of the dew, sun and moon are our cousins, and the stars, they're just children we'd like to seed our wombs with. And after all, what's so great about being one of the book-people? They don't know the secret of life, or how to fill hearts with songs and laughing, and how to share somebody else's loneliness."

Couvade paused and raised her hands in a self-deprecating gesture. "But look at how I filling up you ears with talk! You see, when Ti-Zek's not around, and with the children scattered and gone, the only person left to talk to is neighbor-Raj. So you couldn't have come a better time." She clapped her hands and hummed a tune.

"Belfon, lemme give you a piece of advice before you settle down to eat and gaff, don't grow up to be a no maku-man, no dreamer locked up inside of himself. Learn, instead, how to open your heart to the world. Atlassa tried his best, but he didn't suck-seed, he sucked gall instead, that's why he had to head for the deep bush and the mountains to hide in, because, don't make no mistake, I love that old man, but Biaro's a sleeper's place, a hideaway, a halfway stop between Atlassa's heaven and his hell, and it can't be that for nobody else but him. When he pass on he'll carry his Biaro to the grave with him, and all we'll have left is the dry husk of a dream. That's what sleepers like him and Father Marquez end up with—the husk of a dream! I suspect that's why he send you away to study, he don't want his dream to lock you up in Biaro for the rest of your life, he want to prepare you to live in the world. I think he even want you to conquer that world, Belfon. That man Atlassa is a lionhearted man, sometimes, he can take on the powers and the principalities in Kamarang, Brazil, Venezuela, Surinam, and yet he never learn how to conquer his own heart. He's been looking for a redemption secret in the heart of every woman he ever met. Boy, it will take you a long time to understand all I'm telling you on this goodly afternoon, but it will come to pass one day, you'll sit down by yourself and all will be revealed to you." She laughed, as she walked past me on her way to the kitchen, leaving a cloying smell of sweet sage, wild honey, and talcum powder in her wake.

"You didn't know I was an honest-to-goodness preacher-woman did you, young Belfon?" she sang out, and her laughter filled the small house and made my heart jump. When she reentered the living room, she said matter-of-factly:

"I'll prepare a little something for you to eat, and then you can rest. That trip from Biaro is a bone-wearying one, and it's good you didn't have to depend on those cookshops in Georgetown which I hear they now calling restaurants, because all you're liable to get is stray dog stew or alley cat chow mein."

"Don't go to any trouble on my account, Couvade," I said politely.

"What you mean by trouble, boy? Since when it's been trouble for Couvade to prepare a little something to eat for Atlassa's godson? Boy, just take off those hot and sweaty boots and your fancy vest, and step out in the backyard with me. I want you to help me catch two leghorn hens I was keeping for a special occasion like this one."

When I left the dark interior of the cottage, the bright sunshine made me stumble and fall over a mortar and pestle at the foot of the stairs. I picked myself up, and walking toward the fowlhouse, felt fresh chicken dung between my bare toes, and this reminded me of childhood days with my mother. She used to keep noisy guinea hens in the yard behind our kitchen, and I always had to step carefully to avoid fresh droppings. Those guinea fowls were good sentinels, raising Cain at any intruder. Our guinea fowls lived mostly on cockroaches, grass seeds, and garbage. Neighborhood cats and dogs respected them because they were noisy, cantankerous, and could inflict painful wounds with their sharp beaks, and if the odds against them were too great they'd simply take to the air; they were vertical take-off artists. I once saw a guinea hen maim a large wharf rat that was trying to steal her eggs.

Couvade's backyard was large and well-tended. It was unlike the postage stamp spaces around my mother's hut, or the vast expanses of forests, mountains, and savannahs around Biaro. What luxury! I mused. Couvade keeps leghorns instead of guinea fowls! She scattered paddy on the ground, and the leghorns rushed to peck at the golden grains. Clustered together, they looked like a huge flower opening and closing its petals.

"That's the two I want," she said, pointing to two full-breasted hens. I seized them by the wings with practiced skill and cut off their heads. Blood stained the grass, a bright crimson, but as the sun and wind soon dried it up, it darkened to the dull brown of old leather. I soaked the birds in hot water and plucked them. Couvade gathered the feathers and spread them out on a galvanized iron sheet to dry in the sun. Later on she'd wash and bleach them, and use them for stuffing pillows and cushions. I buried the entrails to prevent stray cats and dogs from invading the yard to devour them. Then I cut the meat into small pieces and used lime juice, powdered green papaya, mint, Marsala curry powder, wirri-wirri peppers, and crushed flowers from the Spanish cordia to season it. Rajkumaria, Couvade's neighbor, called out:

"Eh, eh, neighbor, like you have company! What a way the young man look big and strong! Young feller, you must be a destroyer of women!"

"Is Atlassa godson," Couvade informed her, and Raj exclaimed:

"Belfon? Is you grow up so? Lord have mercy! I used to know you when you was a small-boy! Well, what a way we getting old, Couvade!"

"Speak for yourself, Raj, people are as old as they feel, and I can tell you, I don't feel Father Age knocking on my door yet."

"Good afternoon, Auntie Raj," I said, respectfully. Raj, who was wearing a brightly colored sari spun around her voluptuous figure like a web, had visited Biaro several times to buy precious and semiprecious stones from Atlassa.

"And how is the old man?" Raj asked, and Couvade butted in derisively:

"Which old man? You mean that old reprobate, Atlassa? Well, I can tell you, Raj, the grave is going to yawn under the lot of us before he decide to walk the last mile to the Forest of the Long Night."

I wanted to shout at Couvade:

My godfather's a good man and a great man, the greatest that ever ever lived. There's none like him in the whole wide world! But I stood tongue-tied because I knew the words would tumble out of my mouth and make me a laughstock before these two older women.

Raj, noticing the expression on my face, commented with a wicked smile, "Watch how you talking about the young man's god." She was tall, in her forties, with a lewd mouth. She looked like a priestess in the temple of Rati. A Hindu friend had told me about these temples where, stretched out on opulent rugs, the priests and priestesses made love as part of a religious ritual, and looking on, the congregation felt transported to Nirvana.

"His godfather had him locked up in the bush, filling up his young head with book-learning, and now, he's on his way to university," Couvade said.

"I wonder why old Atlassa never lived in town. Me, I'm a town person, when I stand up outdoors I like to feel buildings around me—trees and sky and hills and open savannahs are not my cup of tea," Raj declared. I could feel her eyes still sizing me up with a brazen and good-natured sensuality.

While Couvade was preparing a meal of curried chicken, dhal, and roti, she hummed and sang and talked to herself, and as if she suddenly remembered that I was there, questioned me about Biaro:

"How is that crazy Englishwoman, Mistress Hailsham?"

"She's all right. But one of her three husbands died."

"But that woman bold as brass eh, living openly with three husbands under the same roof! There's an advantage to having three husbands at the same time, because, if Mantop snatch one of them away then you have two left. Which one of the three passed away?"

"Matawa, the Wai-Wai chief."

"I remember him. He was a big man with a scar like a new moon shining on his forehead. And Mistress Hailsham still running the school?"

"Yes."

"And how Beltina faring these days?"

"I don't understand, Couvade."

"I mean, is she looking well? You notice any gray hairs on her head?"

"She has some around the temples, but her face hasn't changed one bit."

"And what about Atlassa?"

"He hasn't changed much, either. It's the same Atlassa with the same slow voice, the same tall slengereh body, the same big eyes, and age only slowing him down a lil bit at a time."

Using her free hand to emphasize points she was making, Couvade said, "Atlassa started out by living life like a river without rocks to check its flow, but now that old age catching up with him, he's learnt to control the flow so that it can slow to a trickle or surge in a great onrush of white water.

"And what about Kartabo, the Shaman, he still living all by himself on the edge of the South Cliff?" Having asked the question, she answered it before I could reply. "But that's a strange Carib man, eh! The first time I went to visit him in his dark hut, and everybody in Biaro told me I had to, the blasted prophet-man kept me waiting for a long time. The place was so quiet, it was as if the life I had lived and stored up in my mind began: drip, drip, drip, and by the time he came out of the darkness to face me, I was floating in a lake of my own memories. And I knew Kartabo was looking into that lake and reading the whole story of my life. After that I never went to see him again because I didn't want Kartabo, or anybody else for that matter, to get to know me too well. It would've given them too much power over me."

When she paused to reflect, I volunteered a tidbit of news about Kartabo. "The other day Mistress Hailsham was sick with fever and vomiting, but Kartabo treated her and she got better. Folks come from far and wide to be healed by him."

But Couvade responded, "I already know about that because Raj went to see Kartabo the other day, and she told me he said all that's wrong with the Hailsham woman is she's fretting against old age, she sees old age as some kind of vulture with big black wings following her, and even in the night that vulture's shadow is there, blacker than the darkness."

I said naively, "Mistress Hailsham says that sometimes the darkness at Biaro is alive, and she can feel it hugging her and breathing down her neck."

There were beads of perspiration on Couvade's smooth forehead and she wiped them off with her forearm. She moved with ease in her small kitchen, and every now and then she'd dance in time to the tune she was humming, and there was a glimmer in her dark eyes when she looked at me. I had seen the same look in Rajkumaria's eyes. It was as if they both had gazed into the depths of men's hearts and found secrets only female outlaws against convention could discover. And this, gave them power.

We ate dinner in silence, and all around us was the same stillness that Couvade had discovered in Kartabo's hut, for my thoughts and hers fell like water dripping from a rock. I wondered what Atlassa had written to tell her about me. On the way from Biaro I had been sorely tempted to open his letter, but had resisted the urge. My thoughts and Couvade's fell drip, drip, drip, and trickled away in separate streams.

After dinner I dallied away the time in the living room while Couvade washed the pots and dishes. I'd offered to help but she refused:

"Boy, you're too big for this small kitchen. Make yourself comfortable in the drawing room ... And since you're one of the book-people, you can look at my books and take down any one of them from the drawing room shelf. Soon join you."

Gaudy parrots hurled themselves across the evening sky and six o'clock bees welcomed the dusk with their high-pitched singing. Couvade had a collection of books on solid purpleheart shelves, and the books, the shelves, and the dust seemed to be fused together. Father Marquez's leather-bound books were on the top shelves. Borers and moths had played havoc with the book jackets but the onionskin pages were intact. There were the collected poems of Robert Herrick; Milton's *Comus, Lycidas, Paradise Lost* and *Paradise Regained,* in separate volumes; Macaulay's *Lays of Ancient Rome; Historia de las Americas* by Las Casas; an English translation of Michelet's *Joan of Arc,* and a French edition of his *Historical View of the French Revolution;* worn copies of Latin primers, texts on English Grammar, and Royal Readers for different grades.

Father Marquez, Couvade's spiritual mentor, teacher, guardian, and lover had comments on the title pages of some of the volumes. In one volume he had written: "Milton understood the vileness of the women who destroyed Orpheus, and the iniquity of their sins of the flesh." His comment of Joan of Arc was this: "A woman possessed completely by the love of God is at once an angel and a demon at large."

"He was a peculiar man, that Father Marquez," Couvade sang out from the kitchen. Joining me, she added quietly, "The sun and rain at Aquero had grilled him till he was the color of mahogany bark. He said he was a Soldier of Christ who swore before God to renounce all the temptations of the flesh, and yet it was he who first burst the cherry between my legs when I was fifteen. He took me for a walk through a field of wild ferns after school, and lying down on those soft ferns, he made the fires of God burn inside my belly. The Carib shamans don't go in for that kind of hypocrisy, they sanctify the act, they don't have to pretend to banish it. The child I had by that first meeting of flesh to flesh is now a government minister and a pillar of the church. And you'd think he's a child of the Virgin Mary because he don't acknowledge me as his mother. Night after night Father Marquez used to read to me, and his voice used to hypnotize me. I can still hear it deep inside my head. After the reading, he would take me to bed and curse women and the sins of the flesh, all the while trying to punish me with his rod of correction..."

"Atlassa never told me a word about his friend's iniquities. I grew up believing that the man was a saint."

"A saint, eh?"

"What really happened to him, Couvade?" I asked, and she did not reply. She had just washed her hair, and was drying it vigorously.

"He was saint and the devil in one body," she mumbled.

I thumbed through *Paradise Lost* and remembered how Atlassa used to chant this poem against a background of Gregorian canta firma sung by Mistress Hailsham's Amerindian choir. The young Amerindians had voices sweeter by far than those of bellbirds, and listening to them always made my heart quiver. Drums, panpipes, and flutes accompanied the choir. These performances were held in a grove of trees at night when the sky looked like a gigantic upturned velvet bowl in which billions of fireflies had been trapped. And in the distance we could sometimes hear jaguars coughing.

He had written on a blank page of *Paradise Regained:* "I'm here at the equator. I see the sun coming up from the same region above the trees in the East every day, and setting quite vertically and suddenly, exactly on the other side, with the same repetitive simplicity. Certainly, this must have a profound effect on the mind, body, and soul."

"Is there any fresh news about Father Marquez?" I asked once more. She stopped drying her hair for a while, but did not look up as she spoke and her voice sounded strange and distant.

"He went searching for a group of Indians who people say were living in the swamps above the Barima since before the time of Columbus...he went with two young Caribs from the Bara-Bara region...the three of them never came back. It was rumored that the wild women of the swamps and hills of Kaituma beatified him with spears and knives, and then they sent his head down the Barima on a balsa raft. Still and all, other folks swear he's still alive. One man swore he saw him in Brazil; a woman even declared he give up the Faith, and is living in the Surinam bush with five wives. But I know he's dead. I heard his soul crying out in the night outside my window, and I knew if I answered it would've followed me for the rest of my days; so I let his troubled soul pass by to live out its purgatory in some other place."

Listening to her I couldn't help feeling regret that I would never have the courage to live life on my terms the way she had done on hers.

It was dark outside. A sliver of the moon grew larger and larger as it appeared above the treetops. But it had no sooner made its appearance than opaque clouds blotted it out. In the sudden gloom, frogs began calling insistently for rain from the depths of the canefields.

"Help me dry my hair, nuh!" Couvade said, handing me a clean towel.

I sat on the edge of the couch while she settled herself comfortably on the floor between my legs, her head tilted slightly backward.

"Father Marquez and Atlassa, an atheist and a Jesuit, what an odd pair!" I said, drying her thick, curly hair. It felt like moss hanging from bearded trees, and I was glad that Couvade was sitting with her back to me. I tried my best to make my voice sound normal when I asked her:

"Couvade, what did Atlassa say about me in his letter?"

"I knew you were going to ask me that question, but I'll come to that in a while," she said, moving her head up and down to flex her neck muscles before leaning back once more. "Yes, for true, Atlassa and Father Marquez are alike, both of them spent a lot of their lives trying to punish women for something they couldn't find in themselves. I'm not too sure what that something is, but I'm certain about them searching for it. But answer this question for me, which is better: light or darkness?"

The question seemed ludicrous to me, but there was a calm and categorical strength about Couvade that did not brook making fun of her when she was serious. In drying her hair, the occasional contact of her bare shoulders built up tensions inside me. I wanted to burst out laughing but restrained myself and answered her question gravely instead. "Light. Atlassa always began his lectures to the Sixth Form by asking, 'Adquid?' To what end? And we would reply in a chorus, 'Per ardua astra!'"

"You see how he fill you head up with all kinds of stupidness!" she said, with a sudden burst of anger. "The man want to live through you just like Father Marquez was seeking to live through me. All the things that Atlassa couldn't do, he wants you to do, Belfon!"

"I love him more than anyone else in life, Couvade, don't talk about him like that. Everything that I am, I owe to him. Without him I would have grown up a stray dog."

"You don't understand, Belfon, I love him too. But he ties you to him with hooks . . . if you try to break away, you end up tearing yourself to pieces. Maybe the hooks sink too deep in you young heart already. You see, Belfon, you say light is better than darkness, that's what he teaches you. Well, I'm a woman of the night. I live in the night, my flesh joins with the darkness . . ."

Heavy raindrops began tapping on the galvanized iron roof like strangers seeking shelter. The night wind, coming from across the canefields and blowing through the open window brought the smell of rain and distant forests into the room. Couvade hurried outside to rescue her laundry from the clothesline in the backyard.

There was a great murmuring and sighing of wind in the trees, and a thunderclap made the pots and pans rattle in the kitchen.

Couvade stood in the doorway with her arms full of clean clothes. Her gaze, resting on me for a while, was alternately vague and quizzical.

"You look tired, Belfon. The rain will help you to catch a good-sleep."

The yellow glare of the naked electric bulb made her squint and her glittering anthracite eyes, mysterious and threatening, peered through slits. Rain was drumming on the roof like a host of washerwomen beating clothes with paddles by the riverside. Every now and then a gust of wind changed the monotonous tempo to an angry hiss.

"Yes, I'd better turn in," I said, although I was thinking that in my teens I used to have erotic dreams in which either Couvade or Beltina featured, and in those dreams we almost destroyed each other with kisses.

Couvade attached two chairs to the end of the couch, tying them together with rope so that my six-foot-six frame could stretch itself out.

I was deep in the throes of a dreamless sleep when Couvade woke me up.

"Belfon, wake up," she whispered. "The chickens keeping plenty noise. Must be a thief."

She gave me a cutlass and a flashlight and with only my underpants on, I slipped through the front door and circled the chicken coop. Switching on the flashlight, I saw an eight-foot-long yellow-tailed snake trying to crawl through a hole at the side of the coop. That was evidently the opening through which it had entered, but having swallowed a rooster, the bulge in its midsection prevented it from escaping. I cut off the snake's head, dragged the still writhing body out of the coop, and threw it over the back fence, knowing that between day-clean and midmorning, carrion crows would pick it to the bone.

It was so quiet when I reentered the cottage, that I was sure Couvade was asleep, but when I started tiptoeing toward the couch, she called, "Belfon, come lie in my warm bed. The early morning dew can give you a chill."

I crept into her bed and heard the songless singing of Shango drums echoing from distant forests, and the heart of the drums and mine became one. The rhythms of heart and blood and drums became an irresistible flux and we performed our slow sinuous dance like serpents in the mating season.

The chickens were neglected for two days and they foraged around the backyard restlessly, cackling and scratching, and grubbing for worms and insects.

Couvade, sitting up in bed, ran her fingers lightly across the surface of my chest and thighs, and she said wistfully:

"What a Rod of Correction the good Lord bless you with, Belfon! It's an instrument of redemption. If Father Marquez had something like this, he would've found the heaven he was looking for here on earth. You so tender, boy, tender like a woman... That wicked Atlassa have his good points after all. At least he teach you not to be afraid of being gentle and kind. Boy, you born under a woman's sign, and woman going to feature in your life for all your livelong days. Belfon, darling, to be not 'fraid of gentleness, and to be a man with your mighty body and the brains you got in your head, is to have a magnet for womankind, and that's more important than the lightning rod between your legs."

The corners of her mouth began to tremble.

"Why are you crying, Couvade?" I asked.

"Crying for the joy of living, darling, for the rush of blood, and for the thought that some day the flow will stop."

"Couvade, what did Atlassa say in the letter?"

"Boy, you can crake like a sick grandfather! All right, I will tell you. He said I should introduce you to the city. You know how he puts things in his own style? He say I must take you into the intestines of the city, that's why he didn't want you to stay at the family house. He say since you will be seeing the city with a man's eyes for the first time you must go to the slums and the waterfront and all the rundown shacks around the burial ground. You must see the beggars, the sagaboys, the choke-and-rob boys, and the children fighting with carrion crows to get their share of the garbage. Then you must see the palaces where the ministers and the big chibats live, fastening themselves like praying mantis on the poor people, going for their eyes first to make them blind so that they can nyam their insides in their own time."

"But he told me all this over and over again—"

"He want me to show you, because I know this city well. Did you count the knocks on my door that I had to ignore since you came? Some call me a whore and make up stories about me, but I am a preacher-woman. When the spirit move me, I can practice obeah with the best of them. When you come back from your studies, you must come like a high tide and burst through the seawall and wash away the miseries of this city. There's no hope for you, Belfon, unless you follow the path he set for you . . . I know the big chibats as well as the ordinary folks in this country, from the President to the young green sailors from the Islands who sail in schooners from Nassau to Bahia, and every woman they meet is a proxy of their mama. But you're different, Belfon."

She made me forget that she was naked, that her dark brown flesh was like silk, that we'd been making love for two days. "Still and all," she said, "I hope I was something special to you." She cut off the reassurances I was so eager to proffer and declared dryly, "Sex is like ice in the sun, it can blind you with beauty, flash and glitter, but only for a moment."

I got out of bed and paced up and down. I had been deluding myself that I was falling in love with Couvade, that I was willing to give up my studies and live with her. But, she had just shattered these romantic dreams like a wrecker dynamiting a facade to reveal the dust and emptiness behind it. The cottage suddenly seemed to have become as constricted as a tiger trap, and I wanted to escape to open spaces again.

"Do you know something? I haven't stayed indoors this long since I was ten, and had measles."

"We must go out then," Couvade said. "I don't want you to feel that I'm locking you up."

I searched her face to see if any vestige of annoyance was reflected on it, but it was as inscrutable as a Carib devil-mask. She got up and stretched with the sinuous grace of an ocelot. I wrapped my arms around her and lifted her off her feet. "Let go of me!" she said fiercely, but she had given me a confidence that I had never known before with women. Her body yielded, reluctantly at first. When darkness surprised us once again, we opened the living room windows to let the moonlight in.

THE BURIAL

"IT'S A SMALL TOWN," MY MOTHER HAD TOLD ME. The Dutch had named it New Amsterdam, and later I discovered on a map of the world that there were many New Amsterdams in the Dutch Empire.

My New Amsterdam was a Sleepy Hollow of a town at the mouth of the wide Berbice River. But this river had been choked with silt and it was no longer navigable. Nature had reclaimed its estuary during countless passing moons.

The townspeople of New Amsterdam, having lost their edge as a busy port and a capital, had turned their backs on the rest of the country and to become a people of the dreamtime, a surfeit of eccentrics. It was as though the sandbanks, blocking the river mouth, had closed the door to the wide world outside.

It was in this strange town that I first heard of Belle.

The gods had been generous with the gift of beauty and a reckless courage they heaped upon her. She was six feet tall and Junoesque in figure. Her skin was the rich brown color of a mora nut. Her voice was throaty, and her eyes could dance with impish delight or flash with anger. She could also fight like a tigress. The most notorious bullies on the waterfront had learnt the hard way not to tangle with her. She'd retire to her room with a full bottle of white rum, and hours later she'd emerge, waving a half-empty bottle, and summoning her resident male companion to accompany her on her rounds of the bars and hotels. More often than not, those drunken binges of hers would end in a brawl, in which she would be arrested. But the police treated her with deference and respect, since it was common knowledge that she had connections in high places. For as soon as bail was posted, it was paid by one of her devoted admirers.

By the time she was in her late twenties, Belle had become the most infamous courtesan in New Amsterdam. She had once interrupted a meeting in the conference room of the Town Hall to take the embarrassed Mayor to task for not paying her for services rendered. Standing in the middle of the large room and wearing a flaming red dress, she berated him: "Freddy," (she called him by his first name) "is a whole week gone by since you had your fun and frolics and promised to pay the next day. Well, seven days gone by, and me nah see a blind cent yet, and the las' time ah send somebody to collect what you owe me, you chase him away an' threaten to have him arrested."

He tried to persuade her to leave quietly. Standing up from his ornate carved Mayor's chair, he leaned on the red mahogany desk which was so highly polished he could see images of himself when he looked down. It was as though some phantom and surreptitious spirit was gazing at him from below and 'tauntalizing' him.

"Miss Belle Trumpet," (Trumpet was her mother's name—she never discovered who her father was) the Mayor said, "would you mind coming back later. There is a special room for mendicants to the right of the lobby." He was trying to speak with authority, but his voice was high-pitched and sounded as if it were issuing from a broken flute.

"All them fancy big-words don't frighten me one bit! Mendi-can and mendi-can't? Ah don't have a clue what it mean, but all I know is you owe me money and ah not budgin' till ah get it in cash!"

The counselors sitting in a semicircle at the end of the Mayor's desk were stony-faced. They all knew, though, that but for the grace of God, this scandal could have been theirs, so they felt a morbid satisfaction that they could go home and pontificate about the Mayor's immoral conduct without anyone pointing a finger at one of them.

The flustered Mayor tried to persuade Belle to leave quietly, but she didn't budge until she was paid in full, and in cash. This scandalous public encounter with Belle, and the furor it left in its wake, made the Mayor's popularity soar. He was elected to the House of Assembly when the next parliamentary elections were held, and he became the Minister of Culture in the new government.

Belle's wild spirit, and the way in which she chose to live like an outlaw in a staid colonial society, seemed to arouse in men an irrepressible desire to tame her. Six-footer that she was, she always retained a male partner of no more than five-foot-six-inches tall. Somehow, these live-in men of hers all looked as if they were cloned and, speechless, they responded only with grunts, murmurs, or monosyllabics to questions she asked from time to time. When one of these partners outlived his usefulness, Belle would simply dismiss him and take on another, since there was never a shortage of claimants to her affection.

Fortunately for Belle, the most devoted of her admirers was Royston Cameron, an eminent half-Chinese and half-African Barrister-at-Law and a QC, a Queen's Counsel, whose nickname was "the Axe man," because of the way he could cut the most recalcitrant witnesses down to size when he cross-examined them.

Cameron never failed to startle those who saw him for the first time, for he had a perfect Chinese moon-face and slant eyes. His affable manner and smiling visage seldom gave you an inkling of his true feelings. He fell in love with Belle the first time he saw her, and, over the years, was content to share her with other men rather than marry one of the respectable middle-class society women. By the time she was in her late twenties, Belle, with Lawyer Cameron as her shrewd and canny adviser, owned several lucrative properties, which included a high-class and very profitable brothel on the outskirts of town.

He had proposed marriage to Belle several times, but her answer had always been, "Mister Cameron," and she called him "Mister" even in bed, "the day we sign them marriage papers, you will wake up the next foreday morning to find that you married a whore, and as for me, I will find a Black-Chinee lawyer-man who was accustomed to paying me for favors, all of a sudden becoming a husband; and the obeah magic between us will fly through the window." Knowing she was telling him the unvarnished truth, he stopped proposing marriage to her. And year after year, passion continued to kindle into flame between them.

Belle sold the brothel when she was in her early forties and she bought an estate on the Atlantic coast of Berbice. It had once belonged to a Dutch planter in the days of slavery. The week after she had moved into the great house on her newly acquired property, a girlfriend from the brothel had said to her, "Belle, girl, you give up being one kind of 'Madame' to become another kind of Madame, and I liked the old Madame better than the new one."

Belle's rejoinder was, "Girlfriend, nah worry 'bout me changing. Is the same Belle whatever Madame label they put 'pan she. The whorehouse mek me see this society from the bottom up, and now that I watching it from the top down, what do I see? The same society, only this one is showing me a different face. So, nah worry 'bout me changing. Gal, is the same Belle."

But the outward changes in Belle's lifestyle were very real. She had a large Austin Princess automobile and a chauffeur, and in addition to the field hands who lived on her property, she retained a housekeeper, a maid, two gardeners, and an estate manager, all of whose qualifications and recommendations had been carefully vetted by Cameron before they were hired.

Now that she had joined the planter class, Cameron, who had for so long been a surreptitious brothel visitor, became a gentleman caller instead. Once a week, and rain or shine, he knocked on her door at exactly one minute to seven in the evening, and he was always decked out in a velour hat, a three-piece suit, two-toned boots with studs instead of laces, and a heavy gold watch chain hung from a waistcoat pocket. If he left by nine p.m., her estate workers would chuckle and declare, "Mistress Belle not in a giving mood tonight." But there were times when he stayed until well after midnight, and he would leave walking jauntily to his car, swinging his silver-headed cane and humming a tune. Then the comment of the onlookers would be, "The Lawyer-man score big dis night, an' Mistress Belle gwine ease up 'pan we this week."

When Belle was, as the saying goes, "getting on in years," a friend had asked her, "Belle, surely a woman reaches a stage where passion can't kindle fires in she heart any longer."

Belle laughed one of her infectious laughs and said, "Girlfriend, I wouldn't know, I'm only sixty-five, you know."

In addition to attending the Anglican Church on Sundays, where a self-righteous congregation made it clear by its collective body language that she wasn't welcome, Belle was a Shango worshipper. She had turned a third-floor room into a shrine with regular offerings of food for dead ancestors, carvings of the Orishas, and with Legba, Master of the Crossroads, pointing to the cardinal points on the compass. It mattered not one whit to her that the upper-class women treated her with a haughty disdain or her neighbors whispered that not only was she a former whore, but that she was also an obeahwoman. To her mind, embracing an African god was a kind of insurance that he would answer her prayers when the Christian Jehovah and Jesus Christ his son failed to do so. But she got her revenge when, with large cash reserves at her disposal, she bought more and more of the properties of her snobbish neighbors who were living on credit, pride, and nostalgia for the past.

Mantop came for Belle like a thief in the night two weeks after she had celebrated her sixty-seventh birthday. Belle had thrown her annual wild party, and after going to bed, she never woke up from her drunken sleep. The party was usually held outdoors, but an early rainy season brought constant tropical downpours that flooded pastures and reefs and farmlands around her villa. Belle had huge tents erected close to the main building for the party. And from a distance, the villa and its temporary structures looked like a feudal castle islanded in a lake.

At first, Cameron was immobilized with grief. He shut himself in Belle's bedroom and refused to see anyone. But Ruben Walton, the Estate Manager, standing at the bedroom door, pleaded, "Lawyer Cameron, since you was the one close to her as bark to a tree when she was alive, you owe it to her to see that she has a decent funeral, and since you privy to all of her affairs, you got to bestir yourself and talk to the undertaker." This aroused Cameron from his melancholy torpor.

When Cameron met with Bastiani, the owner of the largest funeral home in the country, he realized at once that he knew hardly anything about the rituals of death and burial. As soon as he arrived at the funeral home, he was shocked to see the body lying on a slab and covered with a thin sheet. With a sharp edge of reproof in his voice, he objected to the careless way in which the corpse of the woman he loved was being treated. But Bastiani, with a broad grin that displayed yellow teeth like fangs, explained: "In this funeral home, the dead are equal, Mr. Cameron— prince and beggar—is the same dead meat. You, of all people, should know how many high-and-mighty ones lusted after Belle in she heyday, and now is only you and a corpse lef'. Lying there naked on a slab, waiting its turn to be treated with embalming fluids. Later on, an old woman will come and bathe and dress the body before the grave yawn under it." And quite calmly, as though it was a trivial detail, Bastiani added, "I can't close the mouth without breaking the jaw, so I was waiting to hear from you or the Estate Manager what you want me to do about it."

Looking at the corpse once more, Cameron saw that the mouth was wide open, and there was a look of horror on the face. It was as though Belle had argued unsuccessfully with Mantop and, with her last breath, had contested his right to claim her life.

But Cameron could not countenance the idea of such a brutal cosmetic procedure being inflicted on the only woman he had ever loved.

"Let her go to the Great Beyond shouting defiance," he insisted, gritting his teeth.

"As you wish!" the smiling Bastiani said.

When Bastiani talked about the price of coffins, he quickly shed the unctuous tones of a Master of Ceremony dealing with the bereaved, and reverted to being a trader in a bazaar. Still, despite the pressure to buy an expensive red cedar casket, Cameron selected a crabwood one. Ruben Walton had warned him that if he bought a more expensive one, grave robbers would desecrate the grave, dump the body out, and sell the coffin with its ornate brass fittings for a high price in the black market.

It was mid-December, and as he was leaving, Cameron couldn't help but notice that the funeral home's front window had a festive display for the coming holiday season. Under a neon sign wishing prospective customers a "Merry Christmas and Happy New Year" were two satin-upholstered caskets with streamers of tinsel, holly, ivy, and sprinklings of artificial snow.

Belle's body had arrived in time for the wake, and Ruben, was there to receive it. The village carpenter had built a catafalque in the middle of the drawing room, and it was draped with bright red, green, and yellow colors—red for the blood-knot that tied her to her ancestors, yellow for endless seasons of ripening grain, and green, the color of the living world.

Ruben, unlike the dour, reticent Cameron, was loud and abrasive and laughter came easily to him. He believed that death should be mourned as well as celebrated, and that the spirits of the dead liked to hear lighthearted and amusing tales told about them when they were about to journey to the Spirit World. It was with this in mind that, as soon as a distraught Cameron emerged from the bedroom, Ruben persuaded him that it would liven things up no end if they held a Shango wake for Belle the night before an Anglican Minister was due to preside over a formal Christian burial service. When the lawyer agreed, Ruben invited a polyglot group of African, Creole, Amerindian, Hindu, and Moslem drummers who improvised requiem rhythms that echoed in far places across the flooded landscape. At the height of the concert of drums, Ruben picked up Belle's corpse and danced inside a candlelit circle before laying it to rest once more. He felt that since she loved dancing when she was alive, this would ensure that she would continue to dance in the Spirit World into which Mantop had ushered her.

The morning after the wake, both the curious and the genuinely bereaved began arriving around nine a.m. Lawyer Cameron, Ruben Walton, Bastiani and his acolytes, all dressed in black, greeted mourners at the front door.

Guests took off their shoes on the porch before entering the drawing room. Most of them brought wild flowers and laid them on the catafalque. This was indeed a heartfelt tribute to an outlaw. The wild flowers, which they had to venture far and wide to gather on the high ground above the flood, filled the room with their perfumed odors.

The great house had been a hive of activity since before dawn. Men and women from the nearby villages had come to help with preparations for the funeral, since it had to take place as scheduled. For even though Belle's corpse was partially embalmed and kept on ice, it would soon begin decomposing in the tropical heat. Besides, ample quantities of food and drink had to be prepared, and all available rooms aired and tidied for overnight guests. Lawyer Cameron and Ruben Walton kept an eye on all of the activities going on around them, but they seldom had to intervene. The women already knew exactly what had to be done. Still, both Ruben and Cameron had one nagging worry. Reverend Jackson, the senior Anglican pastor in the Capital, and Belle's lifelong friend, had sent a message to say that he was ill, and would be unable to make the journey. Instead, he was sending his assistant, the Reverend Grantham, in his place.

Taking Ruben aside, Cameron voiced his concern when he said, "I don't know what this Parson Grantham is like, but I hope he can put Belle's wild spirit to rest."

Heavy morning downpours and Atlantic high tides had raised the level of the floodwaters by the time the funeral service was about to begin. The gravediggers had long been hard at work. They had reclaimed an eight-by-six-foot patch of land from the flood by driving sturdy uprights into the soft earth, boxing it in with groove-and-tongue boards, caulking the cracks with wild cotton and tar, then pumping the water out. The old tombs in the family graveyard stood several feet above the water level, and a profusion of wild blackberry vines bursting through them had scrawled crazy traceries across their stone facades. These fractured tombstones were mute reminders of the high-and-mighty planters who once owned the estate. How ironical it was that they should now be sharing a final resting place with Belle, the great-great-granddaughter of a slave!

The afternoon sun, as though paying its final respects to Belle, striped the still amber water with the shadows of royal, and coconut palms, tamarind, mango, and hog plum trees. Chickens had sought refuge on rooftops of barns and the branches of distant mango trees where the leghorns, sensay hens, and the roosters with their blood-red cock's combs looked like wilted flowers. Every now and then one of them, overcome with cramp, fell into the water, and as soon as it broke the surface, a waiting alligator snatched it up.

Reverend Grantham arrived in time. After a short rest on a sofa, he emerged wearing his ceremonial priestly robes. He boarded a flat-bottomed punt, and from a distance, some devout worshippers who were steeped in biblical lore thought that he looked like Christ walking on water. Reverend Grantham followed the liturgy for a burial on land, but looking at the vast expanse of water around him, he decided to switch to a service for burial 'at sea.' The mourners, some of whom had been shedding a surfeit of ritual tears, crowded around the minister in a flotilla of punts and canoes.

The gravediggers, with eyes red as flame flowers from drinking the raw alcohol that the family had provided, were standing naked to the waist inside the muddy enclosure they had created. Any water that seeped in had to be instantly pumped out so a reasonably dry grave could receive its new tenant. When the casket was lowered into the grave, earth was hastily heaped on top of it, but once the lid had been nailed down, it had become airtight. So, with less density than the soft mud heaped on top of it, the casket refused to stay down, and pushed its way to the surface with much gurgling and flatulence.

A market woman—a professional mourner—who, all along, had been pulling at her hair and garments and calling on the Almighty to forgive Belle her many sins, seeing the casket rising out of the mud as if pulled by invisible hands, uttered a piercing scream and fell overboard. At the same time there was the ominous sound of noisy bubbles coming from the grave. There was a collective gasp, and loud cries of "Lord, have mercy on us!" Some of the mourners crossed themselves, and panic would have set in if the young parson's assistant, a schoolmaster with a stentorian voice, had not called the agitated and noisy ones to order. The echo of his voice had barely died away when suddenly, the airtight coffin shot into the air. Many of the mourners fled, and the speed with which some of them paddled or poled their boats could've won them prizes in a boat race. Others stumbled and fell on the high ground leading away from the house, but they picked themselves up with surprising alacrity and continued their flight. Only the brave ones and close friends of the deceased remained. The lid had flown open and the body had fallen face down in the flower-strewn mud. Employees at the funeral home had stolen the beaded, satin dress that Cameron had provided for Belle to wear on her final journey. Under layers of flowers, she was wearing only a cheap knee-length calico smock, her bottom and legs exposed for all to see.

Sheets were brought from the villa hastily and wrapped around the corpse like swaddling clothes. And this time, the gravediggers, with an intuitive under-standing of the laws of physics, set about making sure that the coffin had enough weight to anchor it in the muddy grave permanently. They did this by placing several chunks from marble tombstones inside the casket.

The young priest, convinced that the liturgy for a burial at sea was inappropriate, began reading the conventional burial service for interring the dead on land once again. The casket, looking much the worse for wear, was lowered into the grave once more, and when the priest intoned in rich unctuous tones, "Dust to dust, ashes to ashes," the gravediggers heaped more mud on it than they had done before. All was quiet after the last strains of the hymn "Abide with me, fast flows the evening tide" died away. Reverend Grantham mopped his brow and sighed.

So, somewhat reluctantly, Belle was finally laid to rest. When the floodwaters receded, the tamarind trees that she had planted years before sighed and whispered over her, while persistent trade winds ruffled their leaves.

WALKING WITH CAESAR

CAESAR WAS A BIG GENTLE MAN with a passion for cars, motorcycles, children, and beer. There was something about him that reminded you of a heraldic animal. He had a large, bushy head and large, slightly out-of-focus brown eyes; his nose had a generous spread, and the nostrils, curving like a crescent moon, could, on the slightest provocation, dilate like a dragon's. His mouth looked like a gap cut into a watermelon. One could call it a generous mouth without somehow describing it adequately. Nature had, on the whole, been prodigal in dealing with Caesar's physical features. He was halfway between six and seven feet, dropping an inch or so, depending upon the kind of boots he wore (he liked boots that exaggerated his height and clothes that made him loom as large as a two o'clock shadow in the tropical sun).

Caesar, knowing he was gentle, always managed to look fierce, and his eyes, which, in repose, were as soft as a cow's, could look baleful and menacing when he pretended to be angry. His camouflage of anger usually worked best with strangers, even though it never convinced the children on his street. He had an original intelligence studded with voids and sudden flashes of wit. He could discuss classical music and appear to be something of that breed of professional colored intellectuals strewn all over London like black confetti; but in the next instant a snide remark about someone Caesar did not like would transform him, magically, into just another ignorant black man. He also had a fondness for inanimate objects, like a motorcycle, a plastic bowl, his tools (when the spirit moved him, he would work as an odd-job man—a mechanic, plumber, interior decorator) that bordered on adoration.

Once, he had punched the driver of a Jaguar outside a cinema because the man had not shown the proper respect for his motorcycle and—just incidentally—for him. When Caesar was sitting on his motorcycle, one was somehow unaware of his boulder-like stature. The man in the Jaguar, about to drive off, had looked out of his car window and said, irately, "Move out of the way, Blackie!" Caesar had taken the kind of swift and bewildering action that left the man in the Jaguar with several loose front teeth—and mostly, he explained gruffly, because of the man's disrespect for motorcyclists.

There was another occasion when, through a friend of a friend, he got a job stoking the boiler in a cinema. For a while the cinema manager and Caesar were on very good terms. The manager, a small fat man, could share Caesar's strength and size vicariously. A Caesar, perhaps, not as dusky as the real one and not as bushy-haired and leonine, became the symbol for the short, rotund manager's wish-fulfillment. But one night, when they were talking about books, the manager had made the mistake of speaking disparagingly of Baldwin's *Go Tell It on the Mountain*. Caesar's face, which, a moment before was as open as morning bright with sunshine, became dark and hooded. Later on that night, although it was midwinter, the cinemagoers complained about the tropical heat. Caesar had stoked the boiler with such fury that the temperature had risen to 102 degrees. But Caesar was gentle, and it was not often that he gave in to his feelings with an excess of zeal.

He had been around Britain for such a long time that when people asked him the inevitable question "How long have you been here?" he genuinely could not answer. He had first come over some time during the war, had served in the Army and drifted back home via Canada and the United States. Caesar hailed from somewhere in the West Indies, but no one was quite sure which speck on a map of the Caribbean archipelago was his island home. He had managed (and this was a unique achievement) not to have friends or relatives from the old country who could remember him as a boy. There were also times when he adjusted his nationality to suit trends in the independence movements. During the forties, when he had occasionally found work as a film extra, and when he had appeared in several films as a naked and magnificently inarticulate tribesman, he had, for some curious reason, claimed he was Canadian, but when the "winds of change" began sweeping across the African continent, Caesar would then claim blandly that he was a Bantu, a Zulu, an Ibo, or an Ashanti. There even came a time when he admitted in a low voice that he was West Indian, but that he hadn't grown up in the West Indies.

In the early sixties he found himself living in a bed-sitting room in Battersea, and it was on a street of jerry-built working-class housing where row upon row of buildings had the identical facade. He had lived in settings like this since he was demobbed from the Army two decades ago. However, in the past, there were regular convivial get-togethers when colonial old-timers used to share communal pots of peas-and-rice, curried chicken, a variety of dishes flavored with salted cod. This highly seasoned fare would be prepared on a single gas burner in cramped quarters where the smells were almost overpowering. While the main course was simmering in a cast-iron pot, he and his guests would be taking generous quaffs of the best West Indian rum, which friends, traveling from home, had smuggled through Customs in containers labeled "Preserved Fruits." And during these sessions, there would be lengthy and heated discussions in which the colonialists would be vanquished and imperialism defeated.

But things had changed since a great onrush of immigrants from the Caribbean had poured into Britain. And in this hectic aftermath of changing demographics, many of the old-timers had returned to independent homelands to hold high office, to drift from pillar to post, to end up as political prisoners, or else to be leaders who, from one day to the next, could go to sleep in power and wake up in exile. And as for the newcomers, Caesar regarded them as a generation of strangers. So he had become a lonely Londoner living in a room with faded wallpaper and with a radiogram and speakers that provided him with the music he needed to banish the nostalgia he carried around like a wound that would not heal. He had an intuitive good taste, which was reflected in the drawings on his walls, some of which he had done himself.

As one got to know him better, one sensed that his was an intelligence that could respond to a variety of tones, moods—subtle reactions that could range from the urbane to the demoniac. He had a collection of books piled neatly in a corner, and several of them were written and autographed by his friends in the literary world. His clothes were packed tight in a cupboard. They included war surplus anoraks, slacks in different colors, and a rare collection of hats, crash helmets and berets. On different occasions, he wore sheepskin-lined flying boots, Polish-made walking boots, and even a pair of Siberian fur boots, which a student who studied in Russia had brought for him.

Caesar's landlord, Mr. Crawford, was a Yorkshire man and widower. He was small, pugnacious, and had an enduring fondness for beer. Since his alcoholic intake began immediately after breakfast, he managed to look pink and florid for most of the day as he strutted around like a pouter pigeon, and he never failed to subject his tenants to a litany of complaints about the rising cost of living and the risks involved in being a landlord. He had been carrying out a kind of guerrilla war with Caesar since this enormous dark presence had loomed in his doorway in answer to a notice posted in a local tobacconist's window. He had reluctantly accepted Caesar as a lodger, and had charged him one pound a week extra. (What Caesar called derisively, a "color tax." But the housing situation for people of color was grim, and Caesar knew better than contesting the issue of that extra pound right then.)

In addition to overcharging him for rent the landlord presented him with a long list of what he could do and what he couldn't. But Caesar, keeping a cool head, paid the extra pound and settled down in the room. When the officious landlord Mr. Crawford (or "Crawfee" as Caesar called him), discovered that his tenant was not the symbol of terror he appeared to be at first, he became more demanding and more difficult. One morning, when Caesar had hurried off to his seasonal job at the Post Office during the Christmas rush, he had left a hot-water tap dripping, and Crawfee immediately gave him a week's notice. Caesar took the whole thing quietly. He was in a good mood because a week ago he had met a handsome German woman at a British Council dance, and speaking to her on the phone earlier that day, she had invited him to visit her family in Munich in the spring.

Caesar was always planning to escape from London. He had tried over and over again and had, with some success, played the part of a professional Negro in Paris, Amsterdam, and Rome. And for a season, he had even been a drummer-man beating out rhythms on bongos and singing Calypsos in a nightclub in Zagreb where the scarcity of Negro performers had made the proverb, "In blind man country one-eye-man is king," come true. But he had always returned to London, to the wide indifference, the miserable weather, to the friends he knew, and to the polite hostility of those who bother to be hostile—for even hostility had a living pulse for a black man like him in a rootless age. But after the landlord's irate notice, Caesar had to find new lodgings in a hurry. His friend Diego, a painter in Hampstead, owned a van and once he, Caesar, paid for the gas, Diego was willing to take him and his few belongings to any part of Greater London. Diego had already moved his friend to half a dozen bed-sitters in the last two years. He knew that Caesar was constantly responding to an urge to move. He was a nomad, always pulling up anchor and drifting to another illusory Harbor of Home.

Diego told him of a vacant double room near to his in Hampstead and he took a half-day off from work and went to look it over. But as soon as the landlord opened the door, he knew that he had come to the wrong place. The man looked too composed and at ease. He didn't really care about Caesar's color or his size, or anything else it seemed.

"I came about the room," Caesar said.

"The room?"

Caesar looked down at the top of the balding head with its pink surface and graying wisps of hair.

"The way this one looks me in the eye makes me know right away that he's not going to waste time hemming and hawing," he thought, then said aloud:

"Yes, the room."

"I don't let my rooms to coloreds," the man said, and then he added calmly, "And for the record, it's not the neighbors nor the other tenants that's prejudiced—it's me!"

Caesar walked away irately but, his angry mood soon passed and with a shrug and a chuckle he declared, "Diogenes, that champion Greek truth-seeker, searched around the marketplace with a lamp for hours, but he never did find an honest man, while here in Hampstead I just step off the tube and in a few minutes I'm face-to-face with one in broad daylight."

CAESAR IN PARIS

IT WAS A LATE AUTUMN AFTERNOON IN PARIS when a mauve sky and a biting, restless wind was giving notice to clochards that the time had come for them to stake their claims to warm subway and office building vents—the hearths of their winter survival. I left the Cité Universitaire early to rendezvous with Caesar, a Jamaican friend. He had arrived at the Gare Saint-Lazare on the London/Paris boat train a couple hours earlier, and after renting a room in a dingy hotel off rue de Rivoli, he had made it on foot to meet me. He was waiting for me in front of a bistro at the corner of rue du Faubourg Saint-Honoré and Boulevard Haussmann, and as I approached, he looked dark and burnished like a dakama tree trunk and strong as the biblical Samson in his prime. He was humming a tune, and this put me on my guard. I knew immediately that this casual air of his was a camouflage that he wore when he was deeply troubled. And when it suited him he could spread joy or gloom with equal facility.

"Something bothering you, Brotherman?" I asked with a deliberate light-heartedness after we shook hands and embraced, and facing me his slightly bulging eyes were like petals of flame flowers burning on pyres of anxieties.

He looked away immediately and walked ahead of me without answering.

"Caesar, man, you're beginning to irritate me," I called out after him, but he held his bushy, leonine head high and ignored me.

I chanted mockingly, "I am the last barbarian looming enormous, a symbol of terror caged in a city, in spite of myself, threatening."

I knew that Caesar heard every word of my taunting incantation, but he continued to ignore me and I shouted at the back of his head, "Caesar, man, you're a rass! Why don't you open your blasted mouth and say something!"

He stumbled for a moment, and regaining his balance, walked on blindly, towering above the crowd, unaware of the people bumping into him and cursing when they wouldn't get out of the way in time. Caesar had never learned to walk on crowded sidewalks without commandeering too much space for himself. He carried the aura of mountains and wide savannahs with him wherever he went. His cold weather attire, too, which he purchased at an Army Surplus store in London, included a sheepskin hat, a Canadian anorak, and flying boots, and this outfit widened his shoulders and exaggerated his height. He started singing a Jamaican folk song in his deep, hoarse voice. A gust of wind provided an accompaniment by sending autumn leaves and scraps of discarded paper scampering with rusty noises at his feet:

"Hosanna, ah build mi-house, Lord, ho, ho!
Ah build it on the sandy ground, ho, ho!
Rain come lick it down, ho, ho!"

Caesar made the folk song sound like a funeral dirge or a lamento, and it left his soul naked and exposed like a stone or a star. I caught up with him and there were tears running down his cheeks and tying themselves like glittering shoelaces under his chin.

"We have a MCF meeting tomorrow. Remember? One you came as a delegate from London to attend?" I reminded him testily, and I felt a sense of vexation almost choking me because we'd been planning this meeting for over a year. But Caesar's bawdy retort silenced me for a while.

"Right now," he said, "the Movement for Colonial Freedom can kiss my arse! I've got personal problems that make your squabbling meetings look like a lot of frivolous shit!"

I knew that at this stage, goading him with reprimands would only make matters worse. Given time and patience, this truculence of his would give way to a more sober and rational mood. We walked out of the winding, medieval rue de la Huchette into a broad boulevard along the Seine. As we crossed a bridge spanning the river, I let my mind stray from Caesar and his troubles.

For somehow, every time I crossed one of these bridges, I remembered Guy

Endore's lively biography of Alexandre Dumas describing how this renowned mulatto had once paid a man to take the Seine's temperature at the same time every day. Once a week, very dutifully, the man would bring the ancient river's temperature readings to his legendary patron. Dumas, Endore wrote, had done this so that this recipient of his largess could not feel like a mendicant when receiving a weekly stipend. And looking at Caesar, I thought, Caesar is just the same kind of mulatto as Dumas, but most people wouldn't know it since so many portraits attempt to straighten that author's kinky hair and whiten his Negro features.

We walked on and on with no particular destination in mind before pausing in front of an equestrian statue. It was green and its rider seemed to be as lifeless as his mount. Caesar made no attempt to staunch the flow of his tears. Facing me, his countenance reminded me of a carnival mask, and I thought this city could drive you crazy. A gust of wind cooled our faces and forced us to close our eyes momentarily. When we opened them, the streetlights suddenly bloomed like luminous night orchids. The bronze horse and rider seemed to come to life and looked as if they were about to gallop down the boulevard.

"Caesar," I said, "I don't know what kind of trouble you're in but knowing you, I'm sure you went out of the way to look for it. Jesus Maria, couldn't you have waited!"

"I swear, Brotherman! I didn't go looking for trouble this time. It just sneaked up and ambushed me," he said glumly, and the night wind seemed to be pushing us in the direction it wanted us to go. Tears made Caesar's face glisten like a polished Dagamba mask under the streetlights, and passersby kept staring at us.

"Jesus Maria, Caesar, control your blasted self, man! Let's find some lonely spot in the Jardin du Luxembourg where your tears can water the flowers to your heart's content . . . and why this trouble of yours had to come on the day of our meeting only Christ-in-Heaven knows. Look, Ti-Jean's faction is trying to take over the leadership of the MCF, and only you can stop them. They'll listen to you and you alone, Brotherman. The Movement for Colonial Freedom needs you! They know there's an undiluted black rage behind your soft voice. You never showed it to them, but they know it's there. They once had it too, but Paris drained the rage out of them. I'd like to believe that it's still somewhere inside me, but deep down I know that I'm just lying to myself."

I would've continued but it was clear that he wasn't listening because he was staring straight ahead laughing and crying at the same time.

"I can't make the meeting."

"Can't make it?"

"I just can't."

"You told me—"

"That was yesterday. A lot of troubled waters pass under the bridge since then."

"A whole year of meetings, plans, organizing—"

"Man, in one day I butt-up with enough trouble to last me a lifetime!"

"Jesus Christ! Why don't you grow up, Caesar? You're a big, hard-backed man, and you're acting like a child!"

"Grow up? It's not a question of growing up, man."

I'd been in a good mood when I set out to meet him, but I was now certain that he was about to make a confession that would upset me for weeks to come.

"We're sons of the night, Brotherman," he said, "and we'll never be free until we conquer the secret fury of the night."

And it was as though my mind had seized upon a wild fantasy in order to avoid sharing Caesar's troubles.

"I can't attend the meeting," he insisted.

Anger almost choked me as I said, "Caesar, Caesar, why don't we escape from these foreign rass-places? We took a journey to an expectation that turned bitterer than aloes. We're trapped in these blasted old cities where cold stones are sucking our lives into them."

"Oh, God, man, you talking all this shit and my woman gone and leave me!"

"Who, Barbara? In England?"

"Who else?"

We walked the Paris streets all nightlong stopping in cafes to drink Pernod until we ran out of money. We tried to buy our last "one-for-the-road" drink with subway tokens but a Corsican bartender threw us out. We joined the night people. Our faces mingled with others to become furtive shapes moving across islands of light. At times it looked as though the faces were standing still while cityscapes were moving slowly in the background. Morning surprised us on a bench in the Jardin du Luxembourg where the flowers had wilted and a single leaf on a tree directly in front of us refused to surrender to the autumn wind.

With the taste of ashes in my mouth I broached the subject that I had avoided all night:

"So Barbara left you, eh?"

"She walked out on me, man."

"You were such a perfect pair," I said, sarcastically, "a Polish refugee who claimed she was an aristocrat, and a black Jamaican ex-heavyweight boxing champion of the Royal Air Force—a Roman lady and her gladiator. So she used you for a season and then she sent you back to your gladiator's pen."

"That's me, I'm him," Caesar said, trying to be flippant. But gloom soon settled on his spirit once more.

"A Roman lady and a gladiator," I repeated, and the confession he had been trying so hard to hold back spilled out with a rush of words.

"Man, after she walked out on me I did the most foolish thing I ever did in my born days, I went and volunteered to fight with the British units in Korea."

"Fight in Korea? You must be mad, Caesar! Don't you know that that's a war against the wretched of the earth? One that's telling us to stay in our stinking cruel huts, and not to get up, not to stand up for our rights, nor to stretch limbs stiff from too much kneeling? What the rass is wrong with you, man?"

"I heard all that shit and sloganeering before, and it don't heal the hurts. That's why I went and volunteered. I didn't have the courage to kill my confused Black self, and so I'm letting the goddammed Mother Country send me to the other end of the world so the Chinese and North Koreans can do it for me," he said.

I answered him by reciting part of a chant of the shamans from my village in the sun:

> "When treetops lasso the sun
> Trap it in a green embrace
> You must leap up to catch it
> And strain sunlight through your fingers..."

"I married the girl," Caesar finally confessed.

"Married her? Married Barbara?"

"Man, I'm one of those macou-men who's afflicted with a soft heart from breast to death. And she knew how to touch my pity. It wasn't sex, although there were times when the sex went to my head like rum; it was the tales she told me about her troubles. Then, last week, out of the blue she said, 'Let's get married, Caesar darling' and I agreed. I didn't tell you or nobody else. I knew you would've lectured me to death. So we turned up at the Hampstead Town Hall after buying the marriage license and taking the blood tests. I had to go out on the street and beg a Greek Cypriot and a Nigerian who were passing by, to act as witnesses. I kept looking for even a flicker of disapproval in the eyes of that clerk who married us, but he looked right back at me and smiled his official smile. Man, I won't lie to you, in that bleak English Town Hall when the clerk was reading out the marriage vows, I felt like caressing Barbara with soft Spanish words like paloma mia, or carazon, because, at that moment, I was sure I loved her. The sun came out when we walked down the Town Hall steps and my heart was singing sweet chariots low. But, there was a man standing at the bottom of the steps, and Barbara said, 'There's Janush, my brother!'

"'But you told me you didn't have any family,' I said to her, but she let go of my arm and rushed forward to embrace the stranger. I stood there rooted to the pavement. They hugged and kissed like lovers, and walked pressed against each other to a waiting car.

"'Thanks, Caesar. Thank you, my love!' she called out as the car was driving away."

"So, she just married you to get a British passport," I said bitterly.

"No man, it had to be more than that," Caesar said, stubbornly.

"More than what?" I demanded, brutally.

"It had to be more than a blasted passport. Perhaps in all the months we lived together, I never really knew her. I kept chasing after a fantasy woman whilst she was a flesh-and-blood one right there beside me. I guess I never had the right lens or the right sensibility for focusing on her needs. I should've reached out a lot more than I did. Then, I swear, things would've been different! I'm telling you, they would've been different!"

And then, he began to sing again:

"Hosanna, ah build mi-house, Lord, ho, ho!
Ah build it on the sandy ground, ho, ho!
The rain come lick it down, ho, ho!
The sun come burn it up, ho, ho!"

EXILE IN PARIS

SUNLIGHT BURSTING THROUGH A SLIT in my velvet curtains transforms highly polished brass warming pans on the opposite wall into twin suns. Splinters of reflected light pry my eyes wide open and interrupt a dream, and as soon as I become fully awake I forget what the dream was about. The two suns shine like malevolent eyes, and my carved bedposts look like sleepless mahogany sentinels watching over me.

I push aside the warm eiderdown and sit at the foot of my bed. The damp cold begins seeping into my limbs, and the room looks bleak and untidy. The brass warming pans have long carved wooden handles that are crossed as if they were weapons. I hold my head between my hands trying to rearrange my thoughts. The cold soon rouses me out of a feeling-sorry-for-myself mood. I walk across creaking parquet floors and draw the curtains. Sunlight floods into the room, and almost blinded, I grope my way toward the bathroom.

The sound of traffic fills the large tiled room, and listening, it reminds me of swarms of bees humming and white water rushing over rocks. The building in which I live is wedged between rue du Faubourg Saint-Honoré and Boulevard Haussmann.

I walk gingerly across the cold black-and-white tiles and stand at the window that overlooks the busy junction. Straight ahead is the Arc de Triomphe, and seen through the branches of naked trees that line the boulevard, it appears to be broken into pieces like a crossword puzzle. Below me, traffic fuses and separates like cells in the city's bloodstream. The Arc de Triomphe, with countless vehicles swirling around it, looks like a monumental gravestone in the center of a gigantic living organism.

My three rooms—a bedroom, studio, and bathroom—are part of an eleven-room apartment that's owned by Monsieur and Madame Renault. He's the Financial Director of an international steel cartel, and she's the mistress of the house. She insulates herself from some of the twentieth-century's untidy realities by immersing herself in domestic chores and reading eighteenth- and nineteenth-century novels. Through her son Roget, she does, however, allow herself to catch glimpses of the century she wants to shut out. She adores this only offspring of hers and somehow manages to reconcile her fear of modernity with his being the epitome of everything modern.

Roget Renault and I are close friends and we're both students at the Sorbonne. Roget, the scion of a millionaire family, is writing a thesis on ancient agricultural technologies in French Equatorial Africa, and I am the first student from Guyana to have been attached to the Curie Laboratories. A recommendation from Professor Bernal in London had secured a place for me in this famous research center. The arrangements suited me perfectly because, working in the laboratory, I also had time to paint, and to take part in the anticolonial struggle.

Roget found my political activities particularly intriguing. It was as if I had opened a window into a forbidden world for him. Before meeting me, he had crossed and recrossed the Sahara desert several times and was only now beginning to notice that the Tuareg nomads who accompanied him had a living culture that was ancient and unique. Writing to his mother about his trespass into new arenas of the imagination also affected her profoundly.

People often ask me what I do in the laboratory and I tell them that I dress up in lead suits and play games with time machines as I measure the age of objects that have residues of organic matter in them. That I'm getting glimpses of a past when human beings were first making their appearance and migrating across planet earth.

I never turn on the light when I cross my bathroom after one of Madame Renault's multiple-coursed dinners. She loves to copy menus from Louis XIV banquets and during these relaxed and festive dinner parties, vintage wines are served, and by the end of the meal I am as close to Nirvana as I can ever hope to be. When I'm flushed with wine, the tiled bathroom floor seems to spin like a roulette wheel.

I often use the bathroom as a studio in the summer because it catches the light from the northwest until late in the evenings. But with its drafty windows and high ceilings, it's the coldest room in the apartment in winter. I tried burning logs in the fireplace a couple of times, but the chimney, blocked with soot as ancient as the building itself, sent smoke pouring back into the room; and for weeks afterwards, a patina of oily grime smeared the tiles, the windows, the bathtub, and doorknobs, and the air smelled musty.

The icy tiles burn my bare feet when I move away from the window, and I feel like an icebreaker parting the cold air. In contrast to the baronial size of the bathroom, however, there's a small washbasin, a miniscule fireplace, and a small bathtub mounted on a platform. With my six-foot-four frame wedged into the tub, I have often thought of how wretched Marat must have felt when Charlotte Corday sprang upon him with her assassin's knife. David's grim and famous painting *La mort de Marat* has imprinted itself on my mind since I began using that tub. It would have been nobler to die stretched out in a Roman bath.

When I return to the bedroom, I hear familiar noises that Evangeline, the maid, makes while setting the table and moving furniture around. (Madame calls her "Eva.") Madame and I have breakfast together every morning, and this is Eva's way of letting me know that it will be ready in half an hour. I spend this time exercising, bending, stretching, skipping, and doing calisthenics to regain the body heat I lost in the bathroom.

Eva is short and plump with a moon-face and dark eyes that can dart from one person to another with the swiftness of a lightning blink. She is a deaf-mute, and those orbs of hers with their ebony pupils serve simultaneously as her mind's eyes and her mind's ears. She was born deaf, and growing up, had learnt to pronounce words haltingly, but after she was an eyewitness to the Nazis executing her mother, father, brother, and two sisters, she never spoke again.

I enter the studio quietly. Eva's eyes and mine make four for an instant. I nod and smile. She, in turn, nods politely, but her look is noncommittal. My presence, in a household to which she had been attached since Roget was an infant, baffles her. Her eyes dart from Madame to me as I make a silent entrance. I'm sure that Eva notices that Madame's eyes are affectionate when they light on me. Madame uses sign language to dismiss Eva, then turning to me says politely: "Bonjour, Monsieur Jan, est-ce-que vous avez bien dormi?"

Madame Renault is so thin that as soon as the dawn cracks, she slips almost unnoticed into the day. Somehow, there are times when she reminds me of a Borgia dagger that's exquisitely fashioned and deadly. The points of her eyes can, according to her mood, reflect darkness, or glittering like dew on the petals of flowers, flash with intelligence in a way that never ceases to amaze me. Her nose is narrow, but it fits perfectly into her small, pale, and delicate countenance. When she's angry, though, she has to raise her head high in order to breathe through the constricted nostrils. She's almost flat-chested. The wind has to paste a soft blouse against her bosom before I can make out the outlines of her small breasts with nipples as sharp as spearheads. Her hair is always lacquered and immaculate. As soon as half a dozen strands are out of place, she goes to the hairdresser. But, she does not try to hide the silver streaks.

"I earned them. These gray hairs started showing themselves early—during the Nazi Occupation, in fact," she tells me as she gently passes her hand over them.

I look at her closely and gauge her mood every morning. She's in a good mood today, as she glides around the table. There's no need for words in this initial phase of our breakfast ritual. We already know each other too well, and the things that are left unsaid between us can fill libraries.

I know that at this very moment Monsieur Renault is sitting up in bed, and between sips of black coffee, he's poring over documents he brought from the office. Every now and then, I'm certain, he is jotting down comments with an old fountain pen in an unbelievably perfect handwriting.

After a pause, I reply to her:

"Et vous, Madame, est-ce-que vous avez bien dormi?"

"Oui, merci, j'ai bien dormi, Monsieur Jan."

The sunshine that woke me up has now shifted to the apex of the building. The ornate structures opposite with their opulent facades have cast shadows that stripe the boulevard.

The splendid Boulevard Haussmann always reminds me that military engineers redesigned Paris, and the broad avenues radiating from the Arc de Triomphe make it easier for the Police and the Army to control rebellious mobs. But between those grand boulevards there are still narrow medieval streets where foul air has been trapped for generations.

"They live like roaches, the denizens of those streets," Madame tells me.

"They?" My first impulse is to challenge her, but I let her continue. Eva flits in and out of the room. She is one of the *they's*, but being deaf and dumb she is outside the pale of this kind of pejorative labeling. I am also one of the *they's,* I tell myself, but Madame grants me absolution since I'm from a distant exotic world.

"Last year," she continues, "one of the denizens of those streets who works for my husband, went south to Menton for the summer. Imagine, after fifty years of living in the twilight, he exposes himself to the sun for the first time! No wonder, that irate sun greeted him with sunstroke and drove him mad."

My response to her bizarre tale is oblique and devious.

"My people respect the sun, Madame, and they know to balance the way they expose themselves to it with periods of resting in the shade."

"But alas, we're crazy sun worshippers, Monsieur Jan; every summer, we offer our pink expanses of skin to its rays. Le suntan is in vogue just as self-flagellation used to be."

"Isn't it peculiar how white people go to such lengths trying to acquire the very color that they excoriate us for having?" I ask, trying to draw her out into a discussion about race. But she demurs and smiles. This is her very decisive way of ignoring a topic that doesn't interest her.

We sit down to breakfast, and Eva serves us fresh croissants that melt in my mouth and black coffee flavored with chicory, served in large ceramic cups with patterns copied from Grecian urns.

"The sun!" Madame returns to a subject dear to her heart, and to show her disdain, she clicks her tongue and continues. "After eight hundred years, Paris has learned to deal very effectively with the sun, too. See how it filters the rays through changing seasons, or else the dawn would come like a big incandescent Quasimodo ringing bells in your head, pushing away the darkness and spreading out bulging arms to embrace the whole city..."

We're on the fifth floor and she watches the sunlight bending around chimney pots and spreading across rooftops. "Dawn is an ugly time in Paris; those who say it's not, sleep through it anyway. As for me, I see it leering at silhouettes it creates every morning, bathing the towers and the steeples and the trees with unwanted light. That's why everyone who can, sleeps through the silly dawn, even the clochards."

"I thought of Marat again this morning, Madame," I say to her out of the blue.

"Marat? What has he got to do with the dawn?"

"I thought he would have been one of your people who detested the sun. I always envisioned him as a man who grew up in a damp basement like a mushroom, inhaling fetid air as if it were incense—"

She smiled wryly and observed rather than asked:

"It was the bathtub again, wasn't it? That's what reminds you of him."

"It always does," I confessed.

"Charlotte Corday d'Armont drained the poison out of him with her dagger and yet, this chaste nun, this Bride of Christ, was such an unlikely assassin."

Madame Renault walks to the window and looking out, shades her eyes. Then, with one of her swift and unpredictable changes of mood, she adds in a voice that sounds almost like singing:

"Mais, il fait beau temps, aujourd'hui, n'est-ce pas?"

"Oui, il fait beau temps, Madame," I acknowledge, just as a mood-swing takes her back to the melancholy business of Marat's assassination.

"Yet, Jean Paul Marat is a kind man and a scholar," she observes, speaking of this revolutionary figure as if he were still alive, and she knew him intimately.

"So we've gone back to Marat, have we, Madame?"

She answers with a nod and continues:

"But he had a blood-lust. He was not unlike that character in Dostoyevsky's *Memoirs from the House of the Dead,* the one who found a kind of bizarre poetry in plunging his knife into living creatures and feeling the warm blood spilling over his hand. Just like this Russian murderer, the screams of the victims during The Terror were a poetry of horror for Marat."

The gentle Madame Renault and I engage in unbelievably bloodthirsty literary conversations at breakfast. We both have a horror and detestation of violence, and yet we feel compelled to talk about it constantly. With my exotic presence in the house and the contemporary Third World novels to which I introduce her, I have opened doors through which her imagination can roam in ways she never dreamt of. She read Asturias' novel *The President* over and over again, and with each reading she wept over the death of Zany, the mad beggar.

"And there are times," Monsieur Renault complains with an amused chuckle, "when she calls out Zany's name in her sleep."

With macabre images of Marat and Dostoyevsky's homicidal character lingering in our minds, I mention Jeannot, a demonic figure to whom C.L.R. James introduces us in his classic history of the Haitian slave revolt, *The Black Jacobins.* Madame has read and reread my copy of the French translation. She tells me that Jeannot is a figure that often appears in her nightmares.

"Jeannot was one of Toussaint's ablest field commanders," I explain, "but his slave master had brutalized him to the point where he had an insane hatred of whites. He once drank the blood of a white officer he had killed in battle and declared, 'I've never tasted a sweeter drink.'"

Madame Renault shivers and makes disapproving noises under her breath.

SHE HEARS MONSIEUR RENAULT coming out of the bathroom. He's talking to Eva. The vibrations in his voice and the movement of his lips covey the meaning of his words to her. Besides, like Monsieur Renault, Eva is from Longwy in Eastern France, and her parents and grandparents had worked for the Renault family.

Madame changes the conversation to banalities. She loves her husband, but these conversations of ours range far beyond the limits of his wildest imaginings. The secret exchanges between us are only for our ears to hear. So she talks about grocery lists for Eva, and how, after lunch, she must go to the hairdresser, and then she asks if I'll be home for dinner.

"I'll not be home for dinner, Madame," I say apologetically, and explain that the Paris branch of the Movement for Colonial Freedom has called a special meeting in an atelier in Montmartre, and I have to be there. But she already knows this. I confide in her, and she shares vicariously in my revolutionary activities.

Madame had once mentioned in passing that the antique table at which we are sitting is worth a fortune, that Monsieur Boloquien, one of Louis XIV's furniture makers, had crafted it in 1660. Then pointing to its exquisitely carved legs, she said that they might appear to be delicate, but they're, in fact, very sturdy. "You can see from the grain of the wood that they were carved from the same log. We had several of these pieces by the same craftsman," Madame said, "but during that terrible winter toward the end of the Nazi occupation, we had to burn them in order to stay alive. And even more bizarre than that, my husband had to ride his bicycle to farms outside the city and exchange my rubies and diamonds for sacks of potatoes!"

In addition to coffee and croissants, I have fresh orange juice, two raw eggs, and a glass of milk for breakfast. Looking on with fascination and amazement while I suck the contents of the raw eggs through holes in the shell, Madame declares, "A child of nature," but what she means is that raw eggs and milk for breakfast are an abomination.

Monsieur Renault walks up the corridor to his room. He wears leather-soled slippers, and his footsteps have a soldierly precision. The corridor runs along the inside of the building and overlooks a dismal inner courtyard. From the toilet window, this courtyard looks like a waiting room in hell, and the neat piles of logs stacked against the walls, like fuel for hell fires. The silence this courtyard encloses is so profound that children's voices echo and die in it swiftly, and their laughter is extinguished like small bonfires in drenching rain. The corridor also runs behind my bedroom, and I can enter it either from the studio or the bathroom. It veers off from the kitchen and leads to five rooms. Monsieur and Madame sleep in the end room, which is as remote from my studio as another country. In the center of the apartment is the library, the only room that is well heated in the winter. A small potbellied stove burns logs which Monsieur Renault and I take turns fetching from the courtyard and climbing back up the narrow winding staircase. There is a big coal-burning stove in the kitchen. Like its potbellied companion in the library, it is ancient, highly decorative, and inefficient. Both stoves have the same coat of arms carved on their facades.

Eva lives in an attic that's within easy walking distance of the luxurious Renault apartment. I caught a glimpse of her coming out of her building one morning. There was an antique shop at the street level and I was fascinated with the fact that all of the objects on sale seemed to be covered with a patina of dust to exaggerate their antiquity. I waved to Eva but she looked through me and went her way.

Because of the acute housing shortage in the postwar years, the Renault apartment should, by law, accommodate two families, but Monsieur Renault is a prominent Captain of Industry, and the Municipal Housing Inspectors do not put him under the same scrutiny to which they subject ordinary folk. However, for the sake of appearances, when the Municipal Inspector is about to pay the Renaults a visit, they somehow learn in advance about the impending inspection, and one of Monsieur's numerous relatives from the Midi arrives and stays for a few days before and after the official visit.

As for me, when my classmates find out where I'm living, they never fail to observe with awe that Monsieur Renault is fabulously wealthy. But I never tell them that the Renaults live a life that is almost monastic; that their sense of thrift borders on parsimony, and that both husband and wife enjoy their ostentatious frugality with a deep and secret relish. They do not own a car, seldom entertain, do not own a chateau in the country, never travel abroad, and spend their holidays with relatives, and the only luxuries they allow themselves are priceless utilitarian antiques and exquisite food and drink. The specter of austere peasant and small shopkeeper ancestors hovers over their lives. Besides, they belong to that section of the bourgeoisie that two World Wars have robbed of its traditional certainties. Two familiar worlds vanished with those two World Wars, and they're living uneasily in a third. Monsieur Renault, heavy with red wine, told me one night:

"Monsieur Jan, the fabric of the world I knew crumbled and disintegrated twice, and part of me was buried in the emotional debris each time...so with what I had left, I walked out of the twentieth century—not forwards, but backwards...into the past...and nothing can ever induce me to look the future in the face again. That Saint-Exupéry had the answer. He flew into the past in an airplane. But me, I walked."

Monsieur Renault is a devotee of Antoine de Saint-Exupéry. He likes his writings, but, most of all, he's fascinated by the way in which Saint-Exupéry had vanished while flying a fighter plane in the Free French Air Force. At the time, Saint-Exupéry was well past middle age. And next to Saint-Ex, Monsieur Renault is a great admirer of General de Gaulle.

Madame gets up, and crossing the studio once more, stands looking out of the tall window. It's nearly time for Monsieur Renault to leave for work, and she's getting restless. "Are you going to paint today?" Madame asks, absentmindedly.

"Yes, Madame, I must finish the painting I'm working on." I reply eagerly, and unveiling the canvas I've been working on for months, words spill out of my mouth. "I'm trying to show an organic unity in the living world by viewing it through my South American forests. A world that forever wears green. And as the Shamans say, when you tear away the green skin of the living world, the earth becomes a graveyard. In this magical but real world, the rivers are the color of molasses, and when I stand on a riverbank, I become one with the sky, the dark water, the rocks, the wild flowers, and the sleeping serpents. This is what I'm trying to show in my painting."

She's not really listening, it seems, because she turns around to gaze at the boulevard. But she surprises me by saying mockingly:

"Serpents in your Garden of Eden...be careful they don't wake up."

"You see, Madame, those early Jewish Prophets were tormented by all kinds of sexual fantasies when they made the man and the woman and the serpent into separate beings. In my Garden of Eden the serpent and the woman and I are one...and the fruit was never forbidden."

I have now won her full attention, and her eyes flash with a sensuous enjoyment.

"Ce sont les mots d'un animiste, n'est-pas, Monsieur Jan?"

"I am an animist, Madame . . . with all kinds of atavistic rhythms drumming in my blood."

Monsieur Renault walks into the studio looking clean-shaven and neat; his suit is expertly tailored, but since the time it was made he has thickened around the waist and buttocks. I have often felt that, like the soft body locked up inside his suit, there are pristine urges bottled up inside him, and they're pushing outwards as they try to escape. His dark hair, with straight parallel furrows left by a comb, is striped with gray, and it looks like white suds at the temples. The lifetime he has spent in offices has left him with a sallow complexion. It is as though dust from mountains of files has been absorbed into his pores, and one day his skin will disintegrate like old paper.

"Madame et son fils," he says banteringly, and greets me with a big smile as we shake hands. Without looking at my painting, he compliments me on it, declaring that it's coming along splendidly. His eyes are dark gray, but laughter makes silver specks dance around their pupils. He enunciates every word clearly when he speaks to me. Between them, they drill me in correct pronunciation every night after dinner. He continues the lesson during the day, but Madame often forgets. To worry about pronunciation would drain the intimacy out of many of our conversations. Monsieur consults his watch, and says:

"Vork vell, Meester Jan," and only because his voice is familiar do I realize that he was trying to speak English. He knows how comical his attempts at speaking English can be, and laughs at himself. We shake hands once more.

"A tout à l'heure, Monsieur Jan."

"Au revoir, Monsieur Renault."

Madame follows him to the door. They linger in the doorway, reluctant to part. I hear the murmur of tender exchanges. It has been like this every working day for thirty years. When he tears himself away, I hear his footsteps as he hurries down the stairs. She closes the door quietly, and does not return to the studio. It's as though she has new secrets to bury in her heart before facing me again.

The sun shortens the shadow of the building opposite. Two enormous shafts of light slant through the French windows of my studio; they're like intangible, transparent flying buttresses held together with colliding particles of dust.

I've have been painting for hours, and during this time Madame has gone shopping, but she has now returned and is preparing lunch. The sunlight falls on my painting from a different angle and is exposing visions from my unconscious that have spilled over into it. It is as though, for the first time my forests and untamed rivers can be seen through a kaleidoscope of the Paris light, the Paris air, the Paris colors, the pink and green and somber gray and brown, the mauve, pale blue, and yellow hues. Then, there's the translucence of the Paris sky; the blazing autumns, and winters when the cold air almost suffocates me; the reluctant spring that slowly pushes winter aside; and summers when a yellow haze filters the sunlight, and moss between cobblestones in ancient streets is grilled dry. Paris fits the seasons of my experience into a spiritual Procrustean bed and increases my nostalgia for a barbaric home. At the same time, it cramps my expectations of ever achieving a synthesis of the seminal Guyana experience and the one shaped by a lifetime abroad. And yet that Guyana experience is like the tapestry of blazing sunsets that collapse into late afternoon skies.

Over a light lunch of soup, salad, slightly bitter Algerian wine, and wonderful freshly baked bread, Madame inquires, "You're sure you won't be in for dinner, Monsieur Jan?"

She's asked me this question God knows how many times. But I know that by repeating it she's intimating that she's anxious to know what happens at my revolutionary meeting—that I must tell her everything that transpires.

"I'm quite sure, Madame."

"I'll leave a cold supper on the table for you then."

She looks at my painting, and startled by it, presses her hand against her heart.

"It brightens the room, and mesmerizes me," she says.

I remove it from the easel and put it in a corner.

Despite the intimacy we have shared, I cannot, somehow, pluck up the courage to tell her that I am leaving the next day for Guyana. So I wait until she leaves the room and, staring at the paintings scattered around me, I conjure up a scenario in which I'm writing her a letter from Guyana and saying:

Dear Madame,

I had to come home again to the amber Atlantic sea and the wide tropical skies; to the swamps and forests and long savannahs; to rivers that vein vast landscapes and the welcome of green hills. Words fail me when I try to explain that Paris, Rome, London, Athens, Madrid, cities where age is worshipped are draining the Muntu, the living creative life force, out of me...

But, right at that moment, Madame reenters the room and I tell her a banal lie:
"My mother is ill, Madame, and I must go home."

Her face is drained of blood and becomes white as parchment. And I feel my heart pounding so hard that it threatens to suffocate me.

"For long?" she asks, softly.

"That will depend." My answer is deliberately vague.

"When do you leave?"

"Tomorrow, Madame."

We embrace. I kiss her on both cheeks, and she offers me her lips. I feel her body trembling against mine, and she murmurs, "You brought the moonlight that you often talked about into my life and it dazzles me. I never dreamt that I could love two men at the same time, until that light bathed me from head to toe."

"The light fell upon me, too," I confessed. "The English poet Byron once said that it was best to love a woman who loved her husband very much, because she loved him more. What he meant was that once a woman has the capacity to love, then it could always spill over and enthrall another."

I'M HOME IN GUYANA AGAIN, and the dogs are restless outside my bedroom window. They converse with one another across the city all night long, and, in addition, roosters crow in backyards every hour on the hour. As if this was not enough to prevent darkness from bandaging my eyes and sleep surprising me, it's the rainy season and raindrops are drumming on the galvanized zinc roof above me with an insane persistence. So, wide awake, I console myself with the thought that it was the same sounds my ancestors must've heard when, in the coffin-space allotted them on slave ships, they had to listen to sea drums for two months or more when crossing the Middle Passage. Whenever I hear the sound of wind and rain drumming on a galvanized zinc roof, it awakens primordial memories.

MADAME'S LETTERS BIND US TOGETHER like hoops of steel. The last one she wrote said: "I thought there were enough living memories to fill the voids you left behind you, but, indeed, there are not. The rooms echo with your absence . . . and your voice caresses me every time I enter them."

Unable to bear this wrenching separation either, I decide to leave the rains, the bright days, the blazing sunsets, and I write to Madame Renault, saying: "Dearest Lucille," (I call her by her Christian name for the first time.) "Although the Muntu is full to overflowing, home can never be home to me again. The bright colors and life pulsing everywhere I turn overwhelm me. Your love for me detaches me from the immediacy of these things, and I know now that I can someday create new and original works of the imagination. When I am here, the possibility of such work is jostled aside. But most of all, I miss our morning conversations which have woven themselves into the fabric of my life and the skein of my dreams. I could talk to you as I had never done to anyone else in my life.

"You must give my warmest regards to Monsieur Renault, to Roget, and to Evangeline. Somehow, I think that from the beginning, Monsieur sensed the depth of the relationship between us, and has approved of it.

"I have booked my passage on the S.S. Victor Hugo, and it will arrive at La Havre on the tenth of June."

Glossary

Apinti a long, narrow West African drum that makes a variety of percussion sounds.

Awaraballi a type of palm tree in the rain forest.

Balata *Manilkara bidentata Sapotaceae* (Sapote family): This common tree produces both a high-quality wood and high-quality inelastic latex. Because the latex (unlike rubber) does not stretch, it was previously used for making machine belting, but has since been replaced with synthetics.

Bisi-bisi a tall weed that grows in the swamps.

Bosey pompous and boastful.

Buckra-man an upper-class white planter, or a high-ranking person of color.

Busha a fair-skinned man of property.

Chibat a male boss-man, landowner, or prominent member of society.

Cofufflement a state of confusion.

Cromanty trees rain forest tree that bears a fruit.

Dakama species of rain forest tree with a dark trunk, which grows to great heights.

Dharu Hindi word for rum.

Douglah person of mixed African and East Indian descent, or of mixed Amerindian and African descent.

Gar-bar a verbal incitement.

Hymara fish large freshwater fish in the Amazon or Orinoco Basin.

Lady's-slipper orchid *Habenaria pauciflora*: a rare rain forest orchid.

Lignum-vitae   a two-colored hardwood (yellow and dark brown) used for making walking sticks, decorative bowls, and highly prized furniture.

Mako-man   derogative term that describes an unreliable hustler.

Marudi bird   large bird of the rain forest that is highly prized by Amerindian hunters.

Mokomoko   a species of plant widespread along Amazonian Rivers with large, heart-shaped leaves.

Pardner   Creole for "partner."

Planasting   hitting with the flat side of a machete which stings, but does not actually cut.

Pocomania   state of ecstasy in the Candomble religion.

Porkknockers   wildcat gold and diamond miners in the Guyana hinterland.

Pragging   annoying and holding up to ridicule.

Rass   a cussword, similar to *damn*, used as a sign of exasperations.

Ruction   abrasive.

Saga-boy   Trinidadian Creole term to describe a sweet man, a ladies' man.

Santantone   light-skinned person of African descent.

Tantaria   aggressive person, bad-tempered, most often directed at women.

Tarzia   an arboreal creature from Madagascar with large limpid eyes.

Tasso   dried piece of beef, like beef jerky.

Tengere   a kind of Jezebel.

Tinamou   one of the big birds in the rain forest. Has a high-pitched call. A favorite game bird of the Amerindians.

Troolie palm   one of the many varieties of palm in the rain forest, used for thatching by Amerindians.

Waracabra bird   a bird that warns the animals in the forest when danger is around.

Wareshi   a basket used for carrying heavy loads.

Wirri-wirri pepper   a small spicy pepper that is a favorite food for small birds whose pepper droppings then scatter the seeds over a wide area of the country.

The Author

JAN RYNVELD CAREW has led a rich and varied life as a writer, educator, philosopher, and advisor to several nation states. He was born and educated in Guyana, and studied at Howard University, Western Reserve University, Charles University in Prague, and the Sorbonne in Paris. In London he worked as broadcaster, writer, and editor with the BBC, and lectured on race. His novels and nonfiction include *Black Midas, The Wild Coast, Green Winter, Ghosts in Our Blood: With Malcolm X in Africa, England, and the Caribbean, The Last Barbarian,* and a multitude of plays, poetry, articles, and stories. He has resided in Mexico, England, France, Spain, Ghana, Canada, and now lives in Louisville, Kentucky.